P9-CAS-623

"They're across the inlet from us..."

Adam handed over the binoculars.

Claire had to adjust them, but not by much. The inflatable boat came into sharp focus. She'd gotten to hate the sight of it.

"They're searching the shore. How can they possibly know we turned in here and didn't go on through the channel?"

"They don't," he said flatly. "They're being thorough. They know they're faster than we are and don't want to chance missing us."

She made a small sound that might have been a moan. Adam's big hand gripped her forearm and squeezed.

Claire took a deep breath before she asked, "What do we do if they turn in here on their way back?"

He kept staring, she suspected unseeingly, out at the restless water. The inflatable boat had disappeared from their limited view, although they could still hear it.

Then he said the words she'd dreaded.

"Ambush them."

DEAD IN THE WATER

USA TODAY Bestselling Author

JANICE KAY JOHNSON

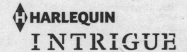

HARLEQUIN
INTRIGUE

If you purchased this book without a cover you should be aware
that this book is stolen property. It was reported as "unsold and
destroyed" to the publisher, and neither the author nor the
publisher has received any payment for this "stripped book."

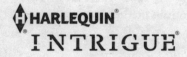

HARLEQUIN®

INTRIGUE®

Recycling programs
for this product may
not exist in your area.

ISBN-13: 978-1-335-55532-8

Dead in the Water

Copyright © 2021 by Janice Kay Johnson

All rights reserved. No part of this book may be used or reproduced in
any manner whatsoever without written permission except in the case of
brief quotations embodied in critical articles and reviews.

This is a work of fiction. Names, characters, places and incidents
are either the product of the author's imagination or are used fictitiously.
Any resemblance to actual persons, living or dead, businesses,
companies, events or locales is entirely coincidental.

This edition published by arrangement with Harlequin Books S.A.

For questions and comments about the quality of this book,
please contact us at CustomerService@Harlequin.com.

Harlequin Enterprises ULC
22 Adelaide St. West, 40th Floor
Toronto, Ontario M5H 4E3, Canada
www.Harlequin.com

Printed in U.S.A.

An author of more than ninety books for children and adults with more than seventy-five for Harlequin, **Janice Kay Johnson** writes about love and family and pens books of gripping romantic suspense. A *USA TODAY* bestselling author and an eight-time finalist for the Romance Writers of America RITA® Award, she won a RITA® Award in 2008. A former librarian, Janice raised two daughters in a small town north of Seattle, Washington.

Books by Janice Kay Johnson

Harlequin Intrigue

Hide the Child
Trusting the Sheriff
Within Range
Brace for Impact
The Hunting Season
The Last Resort
Cold Case Flashbacks
Dead in the Water

Visit the Author Profile page at Harlequin.com.

CAST OF CHARACTERS

Claire Holland—Claire loved sea kayaking...until a brutal scene compels her to save the life of a stranger who could well be a criminal, even if he claims otherwise. To keep surviving, they need each other—but how can she be falling in love with a man who remains a mystery?

Adam Taylor—An undercover DEA agent, Adam discovers the shipment of illegal drugs aboard this ship contains something terrifyingly dangerous. Shot and dumped into the frigid waters off the Canadian coast before he can get word out, he's rescued by a courageous woman who must doubt his story. He has to trust her, but why would she trust him?

Mike Maguire—Claire's friend and kayaking partner, Mike never imagined this trip might be his last.

Dwayne Travers—On edge because he'd taken a hefty payment to smuggle a bomb-making component in addition to drugs, Dwayne decides to ditch the new guy on his crew—permanently.

Lee Boyden and Curt Gibbons—The two men can't figure out why their boss is so desperate to be sure Adam really is dead. Once they discover he somehow survived, they don't dare report back until they've finished the job.

Chapter One

Claire Holland cautiously separated the flaps of her tent to look out. At least there was no patter of rain, but after two cold, foggy days of paddling while battling ocean swells, she was ready for dry and warm.

She and her partner, Mike Maguire, had chosen to follow the western shore of Calvert Island off the coast of British Columbia, Canada, unshielded from the open Pacific Ocean, and it had been all the challenge any sea kayaker could wish. A brutal headwind had been followed by ten-foot-high ocean swells as they crossed Hakai Passage. Claire had been immensely grateful for last night's campsite above a beautiful sandy beach on Triquet Island.

She blinked at the view outside her tent. Sunshine, dazzling her eyes.

As was the case on most of the BC coast, the setting was glorious. The wooded arms of the inlet wrapped around them, and they could see a cluster of the small rocky islets that dotted the short stretches of water between these islands, creating a maze of narrow passages. The air was salty, but she could smell the sharp tang of the spruce and cedar trees a few feet away.

Mike crawled out of his own tent and grinned as he rose to his feet and stretched his lanky body. "Wow. Maybe we should camp here for a week or two. We don't have to tell people we didn't really get to Goose Island."

She laughed. "What say we dawdle, at least?"

So that's what they did while they waited for high tide, which made launching a lot easier anyway. No hauling their heavily loaded kayaks—or their kayaks and then their gear—across the distance exposed by the low tide.

After a breakfast of oatmeal and coffee, Claire happily shed several layers of clothes to bask in almost-warm sunshine—this was only June, after all—while they waited for the tide to rise. She and Mike laid damp clothing and gear out to dry and indulged in an extra cup of coffee.

Today, all they planned to do anyway was wander. Both had paddled most of the Inside Passage from Washington State to Alaska before, although not together. For this trip, they'd agreed to check out some of the most scenic and less-traveled groups of islands on the coast, and catch the ferry home from Prince Rupert in Alaska, just over the border from Canada.

"Hate to say it, Claire," Mike said, nodding toward the shore.

She made a face at him. She'd already broken down her tent and rolled her sleeping bag, but still had to pack up the camp stove and minimal pans and dishes. Plus, they'd spread out more than usual.

They'd met at a kayaking class that she'd taken to strengthen her skills so that she could tackle more adventurous trips. Having been paired up for some drills, they'd gotten along well. After the class ended, they took day trips, then weekend explorations in the San Juan Islands and the Canadian gulf coast islands. Fortunately, Claire and Mike's wife, Shelby, hit it off right away. She was lucky Mike's wife let her "borrow" him, as Shelby put it. Shelby, who liked to sun herself on a beach in the Caribbean or Hawaii but hated getting cold or dirty, was perfectly willing to loan out her husband for the totally insane hobby he and Claire shared. As far as Claire could tell, Shelby had never had a moment of worry about the two of them together, isolated, off for weeks on this journey.

Claire wrinkled her nose at the thought. Gee, the fact that Shelby was stunningly beautiful and possessed eye-popping curves might have something to do with it. Mike was madly in love with his wife, too, or Claire wouldn't have agreed to this jaunt.

Thank goodness she no longer had to worry about what Devin—or any man, for that matter—thought.

Long practice allowed both to stuff their dry bags quickly, leaving air in them to increase buoyancy, and jam their possessions into their kayaks, lighter items at the stern and bow, heavier things like the tent, food bags and water close to the cockpit. The worst part, as far as she was concerned, was suiting up for another day on the water. She thought every time about the oft-used image of sticking your hand in a bucketful of worms. The inside of her wet suit was always clammy. And, even more fun, she had to squirm and contort to pull the stretchy neoprene over her body and get her arms inserted into the sleeves and her feet into the molded booties. With the day so pleasant and their plans so unambitious, she almost tucked away her gloves rather than wearing them, but then looked ruefully at her hands. She'd acquired a few blisters that had popped, and, gee, the rash from the devil's club she'd encountered two days ago still burned.

Oh, fine. On with the gloves.

Once suited up, she reminded herself how

happy she was on the water in her sleek blue Boréal Design Baffin Series kayak. She'd found much-needed peace and self-confidence in exploring the wilderness in her watercraft.

After she and Mike took turns slipping into the cold ocean, Claire looked around with pleasure. The water was almost completely still, a deceptive blue shimmer disguising the strength of tides and currents beneath. She barely had to dip her paddle in to send her kayak gliding forward. Those islets topped by stunted trees blocked much of the view ahead as they emerged from the long cove that sheltered last night's camp spot and zigzagged among the cluster of islands.

They hadn't seen another soul in days, only larger ships out on Queen Charlotte Sound and cabin cruisers and fishing boats at a distance when they crossed Hakai Passage, so it was a surprise twenty minutes later to hear voices carrying over the water. Probably, they came from one of those cabin cruisers or fishing boats whose skipper had chosen to anchor here. Larger boats kept their distance from the intricate maze of islands, inlets and passages in this part of the British Columbia Queens Sound, a small slice of the vast Queen Charlotte Sound that was cluttered with tiny islands on this western edge of the BC coast. Charts weren't always accurate.

Mike was ahead when he passed an islet almost large enough to classify as an island, although it was unlikely to have ever been named. She heard him say, "What the—"

Some instinct had her back paddling, although she'd already glided forward enough to see what had startled him: an older coastal freighter, probably no more than forty or fifty meters long but still wildly out of place. A crane on its forward deck was currently swinging a pallet of something heavy onto the smaller deck of a shining white yacht. Men were working aboard both yacht and freighter, neither of which would be able to linger here long with the tide already ebbing. And why they'd tucked themselves in among tiny islands— No, she thought slowly. They must want to be unseen. She'd read that smuggling was common across both the land and water borders between Canada and the US. People, drugs, who knew what else.

Mike's neon-red-and-orange kayak moved well into the open, even though he wasn't paddling. The frightened instinct telling her that neither ship belonged here kept Claire hovering in the shelter of the islet. Wispy branches of a twisted cedar hung low enough she was able to reach up and grab one to hold herself in place, her kayak bumping and scraping along the vertical rocks as the nearly unseen waves lifted and dropped. Through the feathery branch, she saw the moment someone on board the freighter noticed Mike.

The man shouted a name. Everyone visible on both the yacht and the small freighter turned to look.

Mike lifted a hand and called, "Hello!"

People tended to be friendly in these waters. Several times earlier in the trip, he and Claire had been invited to have dinner aboard one large cabin cruiser or another, most recently enjoying a wide-ranging conversation with a retired couple who said they spent most summers cruising between the San Juan Islands and Alaska.

But this—

Horror filled her chest when one of the men on the freighter lifted a rifle.

Mike saw, thrust his paddle into the water to push backward. Stunned, Claire was still watching the guy with the rifle when a *crack*, *crack*, *crack* nearly deafened her, and something skimmed the water only a few feet from her kayak.

A bullet.

Events had become slow-motion. Mike jerked, then slumped sideways. His weight carried his kayak into a roll. To hide in the water, she prayed, but he didn't reemerge. Untethered, his paddle drifted loose on the surface. Hull up, the kayak floated at the mercy of the tide.

Even as she whispered, "Please, please, please," Claire fumbled in her day hatch for the SPOT satellite tracker with the panic button that would bring help.

But not soon enough, not for Mike.

No, he'd only dropped his paddle and was snatching at something as he rolled. He'd freed himself from the cockpit and was swimming underwater, trying to reach the sanctuary of one of the islets. She'd hear a splash any minute.

Her hands felt clumsy. She couldn't look away from his overturned kayak.

Suddenly, she was juggling with the small electronic device. It slipped from her hand, bounced once off the glossy surface of the deck of her kayak and fell into the water. She grabbed for it, almost unbalancing the kayak, and missed. "Please" was supplanted by "Dear, God. Oh, Lord. Oh, no."

Claire lifted a terrified gaze to see that the crane had swung back into place on the freighter and the yacht was in motion. It turned in a tight circle to pass between two small islands and flee south. She couldn't make out the black letters on the bow. What was wrong with her vision?

Claire swiped angrily at her eyes, and realized she was crying.

RICK BECKMAN SPUN toward the shooter. "Why in the hell did you do that?"

Dwayne Peterson—although probably none of them used a real name—turned a scathing look on Rick. Dwayne cradled the Remington in his meaty arms. "We can't have a witness."

"A lone kayaker? Really? If we'd exchanged waves and a few friendly words with him, he'd have gone on his way without giving us a second thought. But what if some other boaters are in earshot? What happens when this guy is found?"

Dwayne's eyes narrowed. "Kayak's upside-down. He's dead. Probably fell out."

Rick didn't point out that, if the victim had released himself from the cockpit, his body was almost certainly now drifting on the surface, thanks to the flotation device kayakers all seemed to wear.

The *Seattle Flirt*, a pricey midsize yacht, was heading out of this cluster of islands to open water, putting distance between the two boats as fast as the pilot could manage without hitting a rock and grinding a hole in his hull. He was smarter than Dwayne, clearly.

Well aware of the five other men watching the confrontation—no help there—Rick kept his mouth shut, but he did shake his head.

"What?" Dwayne snarled.

Rick shrugged and raised his voice enough to

be heard by everyone. "If any of us get arrested now, we'll go down for murder."

"I don't like your attitude."

Rick didn't take his eyes off his nominal boss, who was bristling as he always did at any hint at criticism. Still, Rick remained aware of the bright red hull of the long kayak floating aimlessly with the current. That poor bastard. Having a good time exploring this spectacular landscape, gets shot by a trigger-happy drug trafficker.

It had happened so fast, there hadn't been a damn thing Rick could do to prevent it.

"Nothin' to say?"

Shouldn't have opened his mouth. He balanced on the balls of his feet, staying deceptively relaxed, ready to move fast. But, damn, he wished he wore a Kevlar vest beneath his T-shirt and heavy sweater.

What was done was done. "Nope."

Dwayne started to walk away. He was halfway across the broad, flat deck when he turned back. "Well, I do. I've had it with you." He lifted the rifle and fired in one practiced movement.

The violent punch flung Rick backward. He crashed against the thigh-high metal curb. Flipped over it. Agony spread across his chest until he hit the icy water, when his entire body screamed in protest. Somehow, God knew how, he resisted the instinct to struggle in the water. He had to stay lax when he surfaced.

Had to play dead.

Odds were, hypothermia would ensure he *was* dead, but he couldn't let himself believe it.

CLAIRE STILL HUNG beneath the shelter of the cedar branch, whimpering, when she heard the next gunshot and saw a man topple backward off the freighter.

Terror and a stinging dose of common sense kept her frozen in place. If she was spotted, the next bullet would be the one that killed her. But, oh God, what if Mike was alive? Waiting for her to rescue him?

She knew better, she did. He'd been wearing his PFD. It wouldn't *allow* him to sink below the surface. If he'd managed to release himself from his kayak and was alive, she'd have seen him surface. Given the shock of the bitterly cold water, he wouldn't have been able to hold his breath long.

Her only salvation was that this storm-twisted tree had reached low enough to hide her and that her kayak was blue instead of a neon color like Mike's.

Tearing her eyes from the hull of Mike's kayak, she sought the *other* guy. The one who just went overboard. Him, she could see, floating on his back, unmoving. If he'd moved since he hit the water, she'd missed it.

A change in the sound of the freighter's engine jerked her gaze up. A moment later, men moved purposefully on deck, somebody securing the crane, others going into the squat building that filled the stern and was topped with a tiny wheelhouse and radar. She did her best to memorize what she saw. The hull of the ship was black with a faded red stripe and significant rust, the pilot house a scarred, stained white. She couldn't imagine the freighter still plied the Pacific Coast with any legitimate trade.

But it was moving, so slowly she first thought she was imagining it, but then it began a wide swing across the inlet to go the way of the yacht. Claire had no idea how much time had passed, but knew that with the tide falling the freighter had to reach deeper waters or risk being trapped or grounded.

She didn't move, didn't dare, even when it passed out of sight behind the islet that was her refuge. She waited, waited, until the sound of the engine receded and something like peace returned to the passage.

Then, she let go of her branch, dug deep with her paddle, and shot forward toward Mike's kayak.

The struggle to flip it was brief. It would have

been harder if he'd still been in the cockpit, but he wasn't. She swiveled frantically in place. He had to have lived long enough to release himself from the spray skirt that kept water out of the cockpit. A spot of yellow caught her eye. His PFD—

It floated alone. He had somehow shed that, too. A dying man thinking he was freeing himself from restraint?

And—dear God—he always kept a small day bag tucked in one of the mesh gear pockets on his deck where it would be accessible. The bag was missing, along with Mike himself.

His body.

She heard a splash, then another one. The man who'd been shot and fallen overboard was trying to swim, mostly with one arm. He was alive.

It might have been smart to hesitate, but she didn't. She snatched the PFD out of the water and laid it across her front deck, hanging it over the compass right in front of her, and then started paddling her kayak toward the only man she *could* save.

His already futile effort to swim had slowed to almost nothingness by the time she reached him. Somehow, he lifted his head and saw her. She had the impression of a bone-white face and seal-dark hair. Hypothermia would kill him in no time.

Bracing to hold her kayak a safe distance from him, she tossed the vest toward him. "Can you put this on?"

He grabbed it with one hand, but nothing else happened.

Rescuing him would be the most dangerous thing she'd ever done. A drowning man's instinct would be to lunge toward her kayak. He could sink her. Flip her.

He lifted a glassy-eyed look at her, and tried to dog-paddle toward her.

"Listen to me. Can you follow instructions? Do you understand what I'm saying?"

"Yes." His voice wasn't strong, but it sounded certain enough to make her think he was still aware.

"I'll back up to you. Climb up if you can and pull yourself to lie flat on my boat. Grab a hold of my cockpit. If you dump us over, neither of us will survive. Do you understand?"

She thought he nodded. This was worth a try. If he couldn't make it, she could go back for Mike's kayak, try to pour the water out, somehow help this guy get in…but he was fading fast. She thought he'd be past rescuing if this failed.

She used her paddle deftly, rotating the kayak in the water, backing up until his hand grasped the rear grab loop. Then she did her best to stay steady in the water as he somehow found the strength to heave himself upward and grip with one hand the rigging that crisscrossed the deck. The kayak rolled to the right; she dug in her paddle to brace it. Left, ditto. Then she heard a groan and dared to turn her head.

Somehow, he'd made it and lay sprawled the length of her stern, sinking it deeper than she'd like. The fingers of his one usable hand dug into the cockpit coaming behind her. Claire had practiced rescues like this a few times, but this man was bigger, heavier than anyone she'd tried it with.

The PFD... She looked around. Bumping against her hull. She grabbed it, knowing he might need it—if he survived the next hour or two.

The speed and liveliness Claire relied on from her kayak had turned into reluctance. It barely moved until she dug in to paddle as if she was crossing an open strait midstorm with whitecaps topping rolling waves, a powerful wind at her head.

She'd been thinking only one step at a time, but hadn't moved twenty feet before her mind cleared enough for her to realize she had no idea where she was going. Was there anything closer than last night's campsite? Besides, it didn't seem smart to go the same way the freighter had.

She and Mike had intended to reach Spider

Island for the night, but they had notes about a couple of picnic stops where they could beach a kayak that were a lot closer. A chart formed in her mind, although with her current stress and desperation it wasn't easy to see the one-dimensional features in the cluster of rocky islands and unnamed islets in front of her.

I should take Mike's kayak with us, she thought with sudden clarity. Try to dump enough water out of it to allow her to tow it.

Her mind was working sluggishly now. Wait. She could call for help on the VHF radio, and rescue would come to them.

"No," a voice mumbled behind her. "They... could be monitoring for calls for help."

They? Fresh horror was answer enough. *Them*.

And...today, Mike had carried the VHF radio.

Thanks to her panic and clumsiness, the SPOT was gone...and seemingly the VHF, too.

Wait. He often stuck the radio in the pocket of his flotation vest. She paused with the paddle resting across the cockpit and reached forward to the PFD. One look told her the breast pocket was empty. She tried to remember seeing him shove the radio inside and snap the buckle closed this morning. Had he not bothered securing the pocket? Or somehow grabbed for both it and the day bag that held his SPOT?

With no answers, her mind clicked to the next problem as if she were watching a slide show. She'd have no dry clothes for her passenger without what Mike carried. Hers wouldn't do a large man any good. She *had* to reclaim Mike's kayak.

She explained what she was doing to the man behind her, hoping even inane chatter would prevent him from sinking into unconsciousness. He grunted a couple of times.

She wouldn't have had any choice but to abandon the plan if Mike's Tsunami had been carried very far away. Thank heavens the tide hadn't yet turned. Maneuvering her own already sluggish kayak the fifty or so yards to Mike's, she took out her towline and clipped it to the carrying toggle at the bow of his orange-and-red boat, fussed about where to attach the other end and finally chose rigging right in front of her.

With a struggle, she managed to roll it enough to dump out most of the water, but quickly found that towing another kayak, along with the deadweight behind her, shifted her normal sprightly skim over the surface of the water to a painful slog. If the waves had been any higher, they'd have been washing over the deck of her kayak, and over the wounded man clinging to life.

She focused grimly. If she were in the habit of giving up, she wouldn't have chosen a sport where the suffering often outweighed the triumphs.

She passed a rocky island on her starboard. But when she neared the slightly larger one ahead and to her port side, she spotted a hint of an opening. Really a crack in the steep rock. If there was nothing resembling a beach within it... Claire didn't let herself finish the thought. She'd go on, that's what she'd do. Her muscles burned.

"You still with me?" she called over her shoulder.

The fact that her passenger made a noise was a positive. If he was unconscious by the time they got out of the water...

Stop. One step at a time.

Chapter Two

Cold, so cold. With convulsive shivers rattling his body, Adam knew vaguely that he was alive. A woman was talking to him. Occasionally, something in the voice suggested she wanted an answer, so with a supreme effort he summoned a hoarse sound. He'd been shot before, so that part was familiar. Turning into an iceberg, he was sure that was new.

Who was she?

He tried to ponder that, but had no idea. The next bout of deep shudders wiped him clean of any curiosity.

He had to hold on. He knew that. Of course, he couldn't feel his fingers anymore, so he wasn't sure what they were doing, even if they were still attached to his body.

She breathed something in a prayerful voice. He tried to lift his head but failed.

Hold on.

Eventually, a scraping sound penetrated his

consciousness. The angle he lay at tipped upward slightly. The surface beneath him—boat?—shifted side to side, him sliding with it.

Suddenly a face appeared before his hazy vision. "Can you move at all on your own?"

Move. Something else to think about.

"Don't know." He tried to form the words.

"All right. Um… I'm going to help you roll off the kayak. Okay?"

Not really, but he sensed she meant well, whoever she was.

This time, he tried to nod.

Next thing he knew, arms came around him and pulled him sideways. Either she'd uncurled his fingers, or he hadn't been holding on to anything after all.

He collapsed on his back, but she kept him rolling until he was on his face, cheek and nose pressed onto a cobblestone street. No, that wasn't right; these stones were smooth but loose.

"Let's get you up on your hands and knees."

Through all his confusion, Adam knew this was life-and-death. He dedicated what feeble remnants of strength he retained to doing what she asked of him. Once he was that far, swaying, he managed to get up to his feet, with her firmly wedged under his arm. On his good side.

"Too heavy," he mumbled.

Whatever she said, he couldn't parse. Not a good sign.

He put one foot in front of another, not easy with loose rocks as his footing. She swayed with him now, caught him a few times when he would have gone down.

He'd have thought this massive effort would have warmed him, but it didn't. They had to stop twice so that he could shiver until his teeth chattered.

At last, she said, "Here," and supported him until his knees touched the ground. When she let go, he toppled sideways and curled up in a tight ball, aware she was rushing away.

Either she'd come back, or she wouldn't.

CLAIRE HAD READ about the symptoms of hypothermia many times before, but always related them to herself. Shivering, subtle loss of coordination, confusion…those meant she had to get off the water, into warm, dry clothes and a sleeping bag.

But this man had passed way beyond the early warning signs. His face was ashen, his lips blue. What little he'd tried to say had been difficult to understand because of the slurred speech. That he'd been able to walk at all had to be from sheer willpower, because his muscles weren't very responsive.

Exhaustion—check. That he was still shivering was a good sign, she encouraged herself. Because that would be followed by muscle rigidity, unconsciousness and death.

And damned if she'd let him die after all this.

This beach was more of a nook than anyplace she would normally have considered for a campsite, but there was just room enough among the tree line to set up her tent, even if that meant flattening the undergrowth. First, though, she had to haul up all her gear, then root through Mike's dry bags for anything useful, then pull both kayaks above the high-water line and probably tie them to trees.

Maybe, she thought uneasily, she could get them under cover somehow. She wouldn't be that paranoid, no matter the deadly events of the day, except for what the man had mumbled.

No. They...monitoring...calls.

They likely had a motorized skiff or inflatable boat on board. Gotten nervous enough to anchor and send someone back to make sure both men really *were* dead.

The merest thought of Mike was inexpressibly painful. The delight on his face this morning as he stretched...

Grief had to wait.

She needed to concentrate on treating the stranger's hypothermia before she did anything else, and for that she needed stuff from both kayaks. She yanked open a hatch and carried several bags up to where he lay, holding himself tight but otherwise frighteningly still.

Thank heavens she'd dried her towel in the morning sunshine. She sank down, cross-legged, beside a man she'd already realized was formidably large. How she'd held him up, she didn't know.

She dried his hair briskly, then pulled a fleece hat over his head, low on his forehead and covering his ears.

He didn't react.

"We have to get you out of those wet clothes," she told him.

Back to yank dry bags out of Mike's kayak and search them, tossing aside what she didn't want, finding wool socks, a sweatshirt and fleece vest, and fleece-lined running pants. Then she stumbled back up the beach.

She discovered as she started to peel off the man's clothes that he'd moved on to the next stage of hypothermia—rigid muscles—and, while he tried to help her, was only semiconscious.

The hardest part might have been getting his shirt and sweater off over his head. Only then did she see a ghastly, openmouthed wound on his back. Dear God, he'd been shot, and she'd forgotten.

This had to be the exit wound. Thanks to the bitterly cold water, it wasn't bleeding, but it would as she warmed him up. She draped Mike's sweatshirt over the stranger's bare back and then ran to her kayak for the first-aid kit.

She layered gauze pads over the exit wound, unwound the sticky vet wrap she always carried and pressed the end over the pads before she pulled it around his side. As stiff as he was, getting it under his arm was a trial. There was the chest wound, a smaller hole, blue against his marble-white flesh. No, he'd taken the bullet more in his shoulder than chest. Lucky for a lot of reasons, but she was glad his brown chest hair wouldn't get stuck in the wound. More pads. Cover them with wrap, then figure out how to roll him.

He wasn't quite unconscious. With her help, he almost reached his hands—well, hand—and knees again, swaying as she wrapped the sticky stuff around twice and called it good. Hypothermia was a greater danger right now than a bullet wound.

The Seattle Seahawks sweatshirt had been oversize on Mike, but seemed about right on this guy. After helping him lie down again, Claire tucked a pile of her extra clothes under his head, so his cheek didn't rest on the ground.

She tried very hard not to look too closely after pulling off his boots and socks followed by soggy, icily cold cargo pants and underwear. She used a flannel shirt of hers this time to dry more of him before getting the stretchy pants over his long feet—had to be a size twelve, at least—and rolling them up his legs. He managed to lift his hips a fraction of an inch so she could tug the pants up. They were too short, but once thick socks covered those fishy-white feet any gap was covered.

Exhausted, she bowed her head. What next?

Tent. Get him inside it and in the sleeping bag, laid out on top of the pad. Somewhere, she had one of those space blankets, too.

Once she was up, she found that and wrapped him in it before she decided to set up her tent as close to him as possible, while keeping it above the high-tide line. She had that part down to a fine art, and within minutes was able to lay out the pad and unzip the sleeping bag.

The tide gradually receded, stranding the kayaks. Before the last exertion of somehow getting him into that sleeping bag, she carried both kayaks up as far as the tree line and pushed them almost out of sight among the undergrowth.

That was the moment when it occurred to her

that she hadn't checked for signs of bear presence. They weren't likely to appear on a tiny island like this, were they? She was almost too tired to care, but set out her bear spray.

Her stranger roused himself to crawl awkwardly, reminding her of a three-legged race—the few feet into the tent. Turning him around would have been harder than turning the sleeping bag so the head was at the back of the tent, so that's what she did. He collapsed onto the bag and she zipped him in, then used the space blanket again as a final layer.

"How do you feel?" she asked, her hand against his cheek. He wasn't warming up at all, as far as she could tell. He got his eyes open, but she doubted anyone was home. She wasn't even sure what color they were. Hazel, maybe?

As if it made the slightest difference whether he had brown eyes or blue.

Focus, she ordered herself.

Get out her cookstove and heat water? Would he be able to swallow if she made tea or coffee? Except, she had a vague memory that caffeine might not be good for him, and maybe not even hot liquid too soon. Warm might help…but she'd see whether she could warm him up using her own body heat first.

Belatedly, it occurred to her that she could have used Mike's camping pad, too. Damn. She could get Mike's sleeping bag to spread on top of them, and then she'd crawl in with the stranger who was no threat to her as long as he was so debilitated.

After unrolling the second sleeping bag, Claire stripped off the top layer she wore on the water, then the neoprene booties, skullcap and wet suit. Even in the near warmth of midafternoon, she shivered until she tugged on her own pair of fleece-lined running tights, a T-shirt, fleece top and socks.

Exhausted, she sat at the tent opening trying to decide if there was anything else she absolutely had to do before she could lie down.

Call for help came to mind, but she hadn't had cell phone coverage for days. She'd dig through Mike's kayak in hopes he'd stowed his SPOT or the radio somewhere besides his day bag or pocket, but she didn't believe it.

The jab of pain was fierce.

Worry later.

When she did squirm in beside the big man and wrap her arms around him, he moaned and burrowed his head against her neck. It was like cuddling a snowman.

Claire pulled the unzipped sleeping bag over their heads to warm the air they breathed, endured his cold face against her neck and shuddered when she lifted her shirt and placed the icicles that were his hands on her bare flesh.

That was not a good moment for her to flash back to the gunshots and him falling overboard. If the freighter had been off-loading illegal drugs, that made him a criminal, didn't it?

How safe would *she* be if he recovered?

Closing her eyes, Claire made the practical decision to push back this worry, too. If she couldn't get him warm, he wouldn't be any threat, would he?

All she'd have to do was figure out where to stash his body so the wildlife couldn't get at it until she could bring authorities back to retrieve him, and to search for Mike's body, too.

CLOTHES SEPARATED HIM from the woman in his arms, and he wished they didn't. The heat she radiated was most intense where he could touch her smooth skin. He pressed his face into her neck and the crook of her shoulder and tried to breathe in that warmth. He slid his tingling hands higher up her torso in search of her breasts, but stopped short. Since he didn't know who she was, that might not go so well. She was toasty enough to make him think about woodstoves, campfires, hot radiators, sunbaked adobe on the other side of the world.

Suddenly, his whole body shuddered so violently it felt as if his spine might snap. What *was* that? When the jaws released him, he sagged with a moan, but not ten seconds later, the jaws snapped closed again and shook him like prey. Was this what it felt like to die on the electric chair?

The woman held him tight, keeping him in one piece as his body quaked and his muscles screamed. She was talking, too, but he was lost in pain.

The first word he caught in one of the brief moments between shudders was *good*.

Good? Deeply offended, he gritted his teeth to keep from breaking a few when his jaws rattled together. He tasted blood and knew he'd bitten his tongue.

In the next surcease, he managed to mumble, "Not good."

Her lips brushed his ear. "Yes, it is. Shivering is how your body warms you."

Or, at least, he thought that's what she'd said.

Wracked by pain, he knew one thing: whatever was happening to him wasn't *shivering*. This was more like being torn limb from limb by an orca or a grizzly. Maybe that's what was happening.

Except it couldn't be, he thought confused, unless he was imagining her, too. Soft lips and voice, strong arms, *warm*.

He didn't remember the last time he'd prayed. He must have been a boy. But he prayed now. *Please, God, don't let me be imagining her.*

CLAIRE STIFFENED. WAS that the distant sound of an outboard motor? Not a cabin cruiser, something smaller. Like the skiff sometimes carried as runabouts on large cabin cruisers?

It could easily be someone innocently exploring from a bigger boat anchored out in deeper waters. Still, she throttled any impulse to run outside and light a flare. She had to wait until the stranger could tell her what had been going on. Those certainly hadn't been good guys on the deck of *either* the small freighter or the yacht. If they were hunting this man, they wouldn't hesitate to kill her, too, if they found him. Just as they'd killed Mike, without a second thought.

If only this were Mike. If she'd found him floating, hypothermic but still *alive*. Tears in her eyes, she thought about having to apologize to Shelby for sharing a sleeping bag with her husband. Instead... Her face twisted and those tears rolled down her face. Instead, she'd have to tell Shelby that Mike was dead. Murdered. That she hadn't even been able to recover his body to bring him home.

The stranger lifted his head with what had to

be a monumental effort. Those eyes, green and gold and brown, devoured her face.

"Crying."

He still slurred the word, but she was pretty sure that's what he'd said. Then his teeth snapped together, and he had another vicious bout of shaking. No, that was too mild a word. *Convulsing* was closer to the reality.

"It's okay," she comforted him. "It'll be okay." She wished she had the slightest idea whether that had any possibility of being true.

Time passed. Hours, but she lost track of how many. Judging from the angle of the sun she saw through the open tent flap when she lifted her head, the sun was dropping in the sky. Given how long days were this far north in June, sunset was still hours away.

The shudders became mere shivers. Color was returning to his face. His hands…felt warm. He was the one to pull them from beneath her shirt.

"Burning," he muttered. "Feet, too."

Wincing, she told him, "That's…good, too."

The dark look he gave her stirred unease that reminded her—stranger. Criminal. Threat.

She kept forgetting as she cradled him, sharing her body heat to save his life. Staying afraid of a man you had shared this kind of intimacy with wasn't easy.

Maybe he could handle a cup of tea now. She

really needed to slip behind a shrub or tree trunk to answer the call of nature, too.

Oh, Lord—what if he needed the same? Was he capable of walking yet? Mike might have some kind of urinal in his kayak…but if so, she'd never been aware of him using it. And…what if the stranger needed *help*?

Claire pushed the extra sleeping bag away so it no longer covered their heads and began wriggling to reach the zip of her own bag so she could free herself.

A strong arm locked around her. "What are you doing?" he growled.

Ignoring the chill his gruff demand had awakened, she said, "I have to pee."

For a frightening moment, she wasn't sure he'd let her go, but then he withdrew the arm. "Oh."

"What about you?" she felt compelled to ask.

He blinked a few times and finally shook his head. "No."

"Good." She crawled out and zipped up the bag again, tugging up the extra layers to tuck him in like a child. "How do you feel?"

"Terrible." He gave a rough laugh. "But better."

"The water along this stretch of coast is likely below fifty degrees. You wouldn't have lasted long in it."

His brow creased in puzzlement, as if he wasn't sure what she was talking about.

And, of course, he hadn't exactly gone for a swim voluntarily. They had to talk, but peeing came first. Getting her camp stove set up, too, and having a bite to eat. Lunchtime had come and gone.

She didn't hear a peep from behind her as she got to her feet in front of the tent and walked away. Clearly, he was past the most frightening stage, which meant he'd live.

And meant he now posed a danger to *her*.

Did she have anything in her kayak that could serve as a weapon? Maybe the bear spray, which was really just pepper spray. Since she'd already set it out, she'd grab it when she got back. Turning, she studied the front of her tent from an angle and tried to remember whether she'd put it inside or just outside. She'd paid no attention as she crawled out.

If it had been outside…it wasn't there anymore.

Chapter Three

He hadn't lied to his rescuer; he felt like garbage. Muscles might as well be Jell-O. Man, his hands and feet especially still burned as if he'd taken a dip in a molten crater instead of the northern Pacific Ocean. Out of curiosity, he worked one hand up above his covers so he could see it.

Yeah, flaming red. Damn.

Beat being so cold he'd expected to die, though.

He pulled his hand back into the warm cocoon and listened for her return. He thought, once his brain worked again, however sluggishly, he would become intensely curious about her. Just now was the first real look he'd had of her face and then body.

Messy blond hair, long enough to be mostly captured in a braid that hung to the middle of her back. Blue eyes, vivid against a face that was as much red with sunburn as tan, and peeling in places, too. From behind, she was slender and strong, but with curves, too. Nobody could mistake her as a guy. After having her breasts pressed against his side for hours, he knew they were generous.

He lay there, rigid, listening for any sound but especially a voice. He didn't like having her out of his sight. What if she called for help? He'd tried to tell her not to, but wasn't sure she'd even heard him. They could use the VHF to call for help, just not on the channel all boaters monitored. Who knew? Her mobile phone might have enough bars to connect.

If she *had* issued a general call for help, their life spans would end shortly.

He should have followed her out, or insisted she give him custody of all electronic devices before she headed out on her own. He huffed. Sure, that would have worked. Given his condition, she could tip him over with a tap of one finger.

He didn't hear so much as a whisper until some small noises out front had him lifting his head.

Seated on what appeared to be a folding canvas-and-aluminum chair, she was setting up a stove at her feet. He could just see her face in profile.

"If you're awake," she said over her shoulder, "I'm going to boil water. I have tea, coffee and hot chocolate. Unless you hate chocolate, that might be the best choice. You could use some sugar."

He didn't have much of a sweet tooth, but she was right. "Hot chocolate."

She didn't comment, just put a pan on top of the flame, then rustled around in a vinyl bag. After a minute, she stood and walked away. When she came back, she had a tall mug in her hand.

From the dead man's kayak.

He labored for a minute over that realization. Was it her husband or boyfriend who'd been shot and killed? Whose clothes he was wearing? Almost had to be. And yet she'd collected herself enough to save the life of a complete stranger. Why would she?

He sat up and, still enclosed in the sleeping bag, scooted himself forward using only his left arm until he sat in the opening created by tent flaps tied back. She didn't turn her head, but her shoulders and back stiffened, betraying her awareness that he was moving.

"What's your name?" he asked hoarsely.

Now she did look at him. "Claire Holland. What's yours?"

"Rick—" He shook his head. "Adam Taylor."

"Not Rick?"

"I've been calling myself that for a while. I... have to think of myself by that name."

She didn't so much as blink, seeming to look right through him. "Why the fake name?"

"I'm a federal agent. DEA. Those were drug smugglers."

"Why were you shot?"

"I objected to the kayaker getting shot." He hesitated. "You must have been together."

She tipped her head back and said in a tight voice, "We were."

"I'm sorry." He wasn't real good at sounding compassionate, but he tried. "Was he your husband?"

"No." She didn't want to look at him. "Friend. I'll have to tell his wife—" Her voice broke.

"I'm sorry," he repeated.

"Why kill him?" Tears rolled down her face when she let him see it again. "He wasn't any threat to them."

"No. That's what I said." He tried to flex his fingers, but they were reluctant. Swollen, he decided. Grimly, he added, "And that they'd now go down for murder as well as smuggling if they were caught."

"They didn't...guess that you were undercover?"

"I didn't think so, but now I have to wonder."

"Do you have ID?"

Her suspicion didn't surprise him. He had to say, "Never carry any undercover. All I had

was a driver's license that shows me as Rich-
ard Beckman." He reached automatically toward his back pocket and realized he didn't have
one. He'd known these weren't his clothes. His
pants... He looked around and saw heaps of wet
clothing scattered around. "I have a wallet."

"You *had* a wallet. Or...maybe." She rose with
a lithe ease he envied and picked up a couple of
pieces of clothing he didn't recognize until she
found his dripping-wet cargo pants. After patting
the various pockets, she shook her head. "Nope.
I hope it didn't have anything important in it."

"A few bucks. Fake Alaska driver's license
and insurance card."

"Okay." She returned to the camp stove.

Since she was occupying her hands by spoon-
ing hot chocolate mix into two mugs, followed
by boiling water, he couldn't tell what she was
thinking.

"How is it we didn't see you?" he asked abruptly.

"I was hidden behind that islet. The one Mike
popped out from behind. I had a funny feeling
when I saw two such big boats squeezed into a
narrow passage between islands. It didn't make
sense, unless... I've read about smuggling. Mike
was too far ahead for me to stop him, but I back
paddled and squeezed up next to the rock where
I could see through some cedar branches."

"Smart."

"As it turned out, yes. Lucky for you, too."

"Yeah." That came out so gruffly, Adam cleared his throat. "I wasn't standing ten feet from the guy who shot your friend. Why did you rescue me?"

Her shoulders jerked. "You were alive. I knew Mike was gone. I couldn't just watch you drown."

"Thank you," he said after a moment.

She nodded and poured boiling water into the two mugs before turning off the small flame and reaching out to hand his drink to him. "Can you hold it?"

"Don't know," he admitted.

He could only lift his left arm out of the sleeping bag. When Claire got a look at his hand, she shook her head. "Uh-uh. It's too hot to take a chance of you spilling it and burning yourself." She set it down on a reasonably flat rock. "Let's let it cool down a little."

He watched her. He thought she flushed, but couldn't be sure because of the sunburn.

"Did you just contact anybody?" Adam jerked his head toward the dense forest just behind the tent.

"No!" Her head came up. "Now I'm thinking maybe I should have."

"I won't hurt you." He hesitated. "I'd like to be able to tell you that you're safe with me, but you're not. You got mixed up in something dangerous."

Those vivid blue eyes widened. "You think I didn't notice?"

He grimaced. "No."

"You told me not to use the VHF radio."

"Did I? I…couldn't remember."

"You said they'd be monitoring any talk. But I don't understand. Why wouldn't they be long gone?"

"They might be." He wished his thinking didn't still feel so muddled. "But I'm afraid they might have gotten nervous. Wished they'd pumped a couple more bullets into me before they left."

"Surely they'd know how quickly water that cold would kill you, if you weren't already dead."

"These guys weren't as dumb as I expected them to be." The job hadn't been quite what he thought it would be, either. Adam shut down any temptation to tell her that part, not until doing so became absolutely essential. "Dwayne will be remembering the kayak floating not that far away," he added. "What if I got to it? He doesn't take chances."

"Thus, him shooting you."

Adam tried to touch the shoulder that hurt. "Guess so. Uh…did you wrap it?"

"Yes. I should take another look at it while it's

still light. I have some antibiotic ointment, but I didn't think to put any on. The hypothermia was a greater danger then."

He grimaced. "Is the bullet still in there?"

Claire shook her head, sending her braid swinging. "No, there's a really big hole under your shoulder blade."

"That whole upper quadrant hurts like hell."

"I do have some painkillers. You can swallow them with the hot chocolate." She reached for a bright red square container marked clearly as a first-aid kit and unzipped it. "Aspirin…no, not when you're probably bleeding. Um, acetaminophen, or I have a few prescription-strength painkillers."

Adam thought about it. "Let's hold off on those. I may get worse before I get better."

She nodded, shook out a couple Tylenol tablets and set them in his outstretched hand before checking the tall mug, apparently deciding the contents had cooled off enough, and kneeling beside him.

He took a cautious sip when she lifted the mug to his lips, then tossed the pills in his mouth and took a lot longer drink, using his own hand to guide the angle of the mug. Damn, that tasted good, and the warmth flowing down his throat and spreading through his core felt even better.

"If you help me stick my fingers through the handle, I think I can do this," he suggested.

She did, then scooted away with what appeared to be relief. Gazing out toward the water, she sipped her own drink, her thoughts well hidden.

But finally she said, "I checked my cell phone. No coverage."

"Have you had any since you left…?"

"Anacortes. I'm from Seattle. And I've been able to make a couple of calls, but mostly my phone is dead."

He nodded. The small city on Fidalgo Island in Washington State was a frequent launching point for boaters heading up the Sunshine Coast and into the Inside Passage to Alaska. Washington State ferries that serviced the San Juan Islands and carried passengers and cars to Victoria on Vancouver Island launched from Anacortes, too.

Up this way, he'd seen Canadian ferries. Waving down one of those would be good, but he'd also seen the nautical chart currently displayed in the wheelhouse of the freighter and knew this current position was at least a few nautical miles from any strait large enough for that kind of traffic or the open ocean.

Then there was the fact that he wouldn't be paddling a kayak for at least a day or two. And *that* only after some lessons. He'd never been in a kayak, or even a canoe. Sending Claire Holland on her own was an option...but not one he liked. She'd be as vulnerable as her kayaking partner had been.

Unarmed, how much help would he be if he were with her?

"Have you heard or seen any other traffic since we got here?" he asked.

Her gaze skittered from his. "I...heard a motor while we were in the tent. Unless I was imagining it."

He waited.

"Something small. A skiff, maybe."

Adam swore under his breath.

"Did that freighter carry one?"

"Yeah, and a fancier inflatable boat, too, that has an outboard motor."

"And...the yacht?"

"Probably, but it's long gone." Unless the load hadn't been fully transferred. He'd expected to see them use a little extra care with the truly dangerous part of the cargo. Maybe it had happened while he was playing dead in the water... but maybe the captain of the yacht had panicked and fled with the exchange incomplete.

Might he still have a chance to keep the delivery from happening?

Not sitting on his butt on a rocky beach that

was more of a sliver cut between the sheer rock walls of this island. The idea of endangering the courageous woman who had saved his life didn't sit well with him—but that cargo had the potential to kill thousands. Tens of thousands. Or more.

He needed to get word out, but he also had to live to do that.

"Damn," he exclaimed. "This campsite is visible from the water."

THE STRANGER—ADAM TAYLOR, if he was to be believed—faded fast after draining the mug of hot chocolate while cradling his hand around it as if it felt better than anything he remembered experiencing. He supervised while she used a knife to cut some branches to further disguise the kayaks—especially Mike's bright orange-and-red one—and the tent. Once the stove had cooled off, she moved it and her heap of dry bags to a rocky spot that was mostly shielded from the water by a boulder.

After dropping a couple of bags, she circled back to the tent to find his head nodding. When she gently disentangled his hand from the mug, he jerked back to awareness and conceded that this might be a good time to take a look under his bandages.

He wasn't quite handsome, she decided, but

he had a strong-boned face with a nose that was slightly off-center—broken?—and a sexy mouth. And, boy, she was an idiot even *thinking* a word like that in connection with him. The odds were not good that he was really a US Drug Enforcement Administration undercover agent. Although it was a clever story, she had to give him that.

All that gave her hope was when he'd said, *I won't hurt you.* In that moment, she'd believed him.

Which made her stupidly credulous. Except... she couldn't have left him to die. She just couldn't. Right now, he needed her. Once he no longer did... She hoped she recognized that moment when it came.

Prepare first, she told herself practically. But not yet.

With him watching her sidelong, Claire felt way more self-conscious than she had even when she was stripping him naked the first time. Now all she had to do was lift the sweatshirt off over his head. She then unpeeled the vet wrap, trying to look dispassionate at having to grope his body.

If not for the puckered hole seeping blood— and a long, thin scar crossing the left side of his rib cage—his shoulders and chest were magnificent. Those shoulders were broad, and she was disconcertingly aware of the powerful muscles sliding beneath his skin and the mat of brown hair centered on his chest.

Yep, dispassionate, that was her.

And, no, she couldn't help letting her gaze lower to where the by-then-narrow trail of hair disappeared beneath the waistband of those too-tight thermal pants. Heat rising in her cheeks, she hoped he hadn't noticed.

After squeezing plenty of ointment in the hole, she placed the dressing over the wound.

"Can you hold this while I look at your back?"

He reached over with his left hand and complied.

Glad he couldn't see her once she shifted behind him, she admired a muscular back very briefly. Then she paid attention to the blood soaking the dressing. Not gushing, but...

"This might hurt when I unpeel the pads."

He craned his neck, but of course couldn't see the exit wound. All he said, flatly, was, "Do it."

They came fairly easily, but she hated looking at this hole torn in his skin and muscle. His wounds needed more help than her basic first-aid training could provide. Given her limited supplies, she cleaned this jagged hole, squeezed more ointment out of the tube, then made a thicker dressing before she renewed the vet wrap.

"Is that too tight?" she asked worriedly.

"No." He started to roll his shoulders, winced and reached for the sweatshirt.

Claire helped him ease it on.

"I think I need to lie down."

She urged him to eat a handful of almonds first, because it was the easiest, quickest thing she could think of.

Then he retreated back into the tent, but did some contortions that had to be painful, judging from the grunts and groans she heard, and turned so the head of the sleeping bag faced the opening.

"This can yours?"

She saw what he held out. Oh, thank God. She took it from him, aiming to appear casual. "Bear spray."

"A bear likely to come visiting?"

"Probably not." Claire didn't like the uncertainty she heard in her voice. "This is a really small island. But there are plenty of black bears around here."

"Grizzlies?"

"Only on the mainland, thank goodness. But any female black bears we encounter at this time of year will likely have cubs with them."

"Don't want to get between them."

"No, you definitely don't."

"Any chance you or your friend were carrying a gun?"

"This is Canada. Neither of us would have been anyway, but it's not legal."

"We had a steel deck panel that lifted to stash weapons if the coast guard boarded us."

"Too bad you didn't have a handgun stashed in one of your pockets," she said flippantly, while thinking, *Thank God he's unarmed.*

Well, except for all those muscles.

"Lousy planning," he grumbled.

"If your wallet disappeared, the gun probably would have, too," she pointed out. "I'll wake you in a couple of hours for dinner."

"Or if you hear any company coming."

Her heart jumped. "Yes. Okay."

He mumbled something else she couldn't hear and seemed to drop immediately into sleep—or possibly a coma. Claire only stared at him for a minute before turning away and going back to her minikitchen. She would have given a lot to take a walk, but thick vegetation crowded right up to the tiny, pebbled beach. Finding this spot had been a miracle; asking for a path perfect for stretching her legs was pushing it.

Besides, feeling jittery was her real problem. It was like having spiders crawling up her arms and legs. Some of the numbness must have worn off after the sugar boost.

All she could think was, *Now what?*

Load her kayak with the essentials, drag it

back to the water and paddle away for all she was worth? Or stay to take care of the man she'd saved and trust that he really wouldn't hurt her?

Could she be so attracted to a real scumbag? Was she foolish to think she could read him, when he was either a criminal lacking any sense of morality or an undercover federal agent who had to be an Oscar-worthy actor?

She gazed at the green walls of the tent, as if she could see through the fabric and into the heart of a man who, whether he was a good guy or bad, had plenty of secrets.

Then she sighed. Getting away at all wasn't likely. Unless Rick aka Adam Taylor really was in a coma, he'd hear when she pulled her kayak from hiding and carried it down to the water—which was a lot farther away now than it had been when they got here. Yes, he was weak…but what if he summoned the strength to stop her?

That was the moment when the noise of a motor reached her—and this time, it sounded a lot closer.

Chapter Four

Feeling drugged, Adam blinked bleary eyes and stared up at the pitched green roof of a small tent. Light filtered through the fabric. The sight made no sense. Where was he? Why?

A hand shook his arm. "Are you awake?"

A cascade of memories returned. Shot. Dumped overboard. Breasts pressed to his chest, smooth belly melting the ice.

He turned his head slightly to see startling blue eyes set in a sunburnt face. "Yeah," he said hoarsely.

"I hear a small boat again, a lot closer this time."

He groaned, gave his head a hard shake and listened.

Small engine, running a little rough.

"Damn." He lurched upright and, to his regret, her hand fell from his arm. Unzipping the bag, he growled, "Need to look."

"I don't know if you can without being seen.

And if anyone is crawling out on the rocks, it's me."

"You wouldn't recognize the men." He scrambled through the opening made by tied-back flaps, having to hold his right arm up to his chest. His shoulder and back hurt horribly. Amidst his other miseries, he'd been able to ignore this one.

Once out of the tent, he assessed the setting. Yes, they were hidden if someone nosed partway into the narrow inlet. If they were curious enough to follow it to its end, intruders could probably see the green of the tent that didn't quite fit in, or a glint of the gaudy paint job on the one kayak. That wouldn't happen right now, not after the tide had receded so much.

Aware of Claire next to him, not to mention the buzz of a small craft puttering somewhere within a half mile or so radius, he grabbed his still soggy boots and started to pull on the left one. Swearing under his breath, he had to ask, "Help?"

"This is stupid." She'd already knelt close enough to wrap her right arm over his thigh and between his legs so she could help pull. "Let me do the right one. But if you fall and hurt yourself worse—"

If Claire Holland was afraid of him, she wasn't about to let *him* know.

She also had a point.

But if this boater—or these boaters—were complete strangers, say, hearty-looking guys in their fifties, he could signal them. She surely carried flares. The boaters could notify the coast guard.

Feet protected from any sharp rocks, he rose to his full height, trying hard not to sway. "Do you have—"

Claire handed him a compact pair of binoculars.

He had to grin at her. "Don't suppose you have—"

She rolled her eyes. "A Remington rifle? AK-47? Or did you have in mind a nice T-bone to toss on the grill?"

"Any or all."

Man, his legs felt like noodles cooked al dente. Kind of there under him, but ready to fold up at the least excuse. The astonishing woman who had rescued him eased herself under his left arm and wrapped hers around his waist, ready to prop him up even if she was six inches shorter and at least eighty pounds lighter than his big body.

"We might be able to get a ways toward the open water." She pointed at jumbled rocks crowded with small twisted spruce and cedar trees, huckleberry bushes and more growing from cracks. The footing looked treacherous, assuming they could push themselves through the tangle.

Adam grunted and started forward.

They never made it to the rim of the island that would have given them a broad view. They did find a spot where they could crouch and get a slice of a view beyond the narrow passage.

The buzzing sound of the outboard motor was enough distance away, Adam felt safe in lifting the binoculars to his eyes. He was surprised by the crystal clear quality of the lenses when he focused across the water to other densely-green islands.

He saw a ripple in the water, followed by the appearance of a dark head, then a second one. Seals? Sea lions?

"There!" Claire said with sudden urgency.

He followed her pointing finger. Metal dinghy, running low in the water. Two passengers. One of the two bent over the engine, but Adam knew that jacket. The other was looking this general direction, using binoculars of his own.

Adam swore and let his drop, not wanting to take a chance of the sun glinting off the glass.

"Two of my shipmates," he said grimly.

"But…they've been searching all day? I mean, I don't have any way to check the exact time, but it has to be evening!"

"Unless you heard a different boat earlier. I don't like this persistence."

"Could they have found Mike's body?"

"And wondered why they didn't find mine?" He thought about it. "I'm guessing they're more worried about the missing kayak."

Or not. They'd worry about a witness, but he knew too much. Yeah, they'd be desperate to be sure he really was dead. Pretty slapdash of them, he thought wryly, to sail away without pausing to hold target practice, using his body.

He glanced at Claire to see her stricken expression. "I should have left the kayak. Except…"

"Except you needed clothes that would fit me, and probably other supplies." He kept his gaze on her face. "We'd have been trapped here without a second kayak."

Her eyes didn't quite meet his. "I could go for help. You're not in any shape to paddle anyway."

Adam jerked his head toward the dinghy, disappearing behind the arm of the island they hadn't been able to traverse. "And meet them?"

"I… No," she mumbled. "I didn't mean right away."

Never. But he only said a milder, "Let's get back to camp, and we can talk about our options."

Claire nodded and rose lithely to her feet. He climbed awkwardly to his own and then would have gone down if she hadn't immediately tucked herself up against him, demonstrating her strength when she bore a good deal of his weight.

"Thanks. Damn, I'm as weak as a kitten."

"Kittens are whirling dervishes. Haven't you ever seen one?"

His laugh was more of a rumble in his chest. "Yeah, now that you mention it."

They made their slow way back, Claire finding footing and then instructing him where to put his feet. Even so, he screwed up by taking a too hasty, incautious step, and felt a wrench on his ankle as his boot slid into a deep crack. She braced herself, patient and solid, while he recovered.

What would he do without her?

I'd be dead, that's what, he reminded himself.

THE STUBBORN MAN refused to take the only chair she'd set up, although admittedly, it was awfully low to the ground for such a tall man with long legs. Still, there was no place soft to sit without moving to the other side of the tent where they risked being spotted.

"I'll get Mike's."

"Don't bother. I'm fine—"

She spun. "You are not *fine*! You're shaky

on your feet, you're hurt and you're stupidly macho!"

She stomped to the best of her ability to the bright red kayak and dug farther in the compartments, retrieving the second sleeping pad as well as the chair—and noting the extra paddle Mike had carried. She'd brought an extra, too, but a beginner was all too likely to capsize himself and potentially lose his.

These intricate passages between islands, so far from any civilization, were not recommended waters for a beginner to learn. He'd have only her, and that frightened her.

One more scary reality.

She returned, unfolded the chair and plunked it down. She had a bad feeling her cheeks were still red. "There."

He gingerly lowered himself, supported the last distance by her.

"You mad at me?" Adam asked.

She gave a distinctly unfeminine snort. "Why would you try to convince me you're A-okay? Unless you plan to take off on your own, you *need* me—and I need to know what you can and can't do."

Very smart. Give him a chance to lie about his intentions.

But he sat quiet for a minute, then gave her a crooked smile. "You're right. With the kind of undercover work I've been doing, I rarely have a partner. It's not smart to confess any weakness to the scumbags I investigate." His mouth quirked. "I'll...try to curb the tendency to be stupidly macho."

"Sometimes I don't know when to shut up." Speaking of confessions. When they first met, Devin had claimed to love her directness. He rapidly found it less charming. He belittled her in front of friends, always with an "I'm just kidding" air that fooled some people, but not all. Then he hit her.

She was almost glad he had. She'd put up with too much, started asking herself if he was right. She was happier single than she'd been having to watch every word out of her mouth. Being dominant in a relationship was too important to some men. She should be *celebrating* the fact that getting tangled with a guy like Devin hadn't left her timid.

As if to echo her thoughts, Adam Taylor was shaking his head. "I want you to speak out. Here, you're the expert. Except when it comes to dealing with criminals who are quick to turn violent."

"If you're the expert on that, how'd you get shot?" Claire challenged him, then resisted the instinct to cringe or apologize. Standing up for herself was one thing, rudeness another.

Amusement crinkled the skin beside Adam's eyes. "You can be really hard on my ego, you know."

She made a face. "I'm sorry. Your job must be dangerous."

"It is. But in this case..." He shrugged. "Speaking of not knowing when to shut up, I knew the minute I opened my mouth that I'd made a mistake. Then I should have groveled, but I didn't. I've seen more men killed than I want to remember, but they were always people involved in the drug trade. Or cops or federal agents, and at least we know the risk we take on. Seeing that creep just casually shoot a completely innocent man who wasn't a threat in any way was a shock."

A fist tightened around Claire's heart, and she bent her head in apparent contemplation of the unlit camp stove. "It was."

"Yeah." Adam's gravelly voice didn't do tender very well, but he seemed to be trying. "I'm sorry. I wish I could have prevented it."

She swallowed and looked up with eyes that burned with her need to cry. "I wish you had, too, except...was it even possible? There were a bunch of men on the freighter, and more on the yacht. You'd be dead if you had, I don't know, tried to jump the guy with the rifle, and then he or someone else would have just shot Mike anyway."

He cleared his throat. "It wasn't a good situation."

"I'm sure you have way blunter descriptions than that."

His smile twisted. "I do, but I throttle that kind of language when I'm dining with a nice woman."

Claire's chest seemed to unclog, and she laughed. "Well, we haven't chosen our entrées yet, but I admit, I'm hungry. What about you?"

"Starved. I could eat half a dozen steaks, but I guess that's not on the menu."

"Nope. Kayaking in British Columbia, I tend to go vegetarian, since I'd rather not attract any local meat eaters, if you know what I mean. Fishing is a really bad idea for the same reason. Mike—" her voice hitched. "He liked to live a little more dangerously and made things like chicken curry."

"You don't buy ready-made food?"

"Some kayakers do, but I cook extensively before a trip, and freeze-dry individual portions in packets. Mike's wife helped him with that, although he's—he *was*—actually a really good cook."

She wasn't ready to talk about Mike.

"In fact, let me go see what I can dig out from his stores. This is probably a safe place to eat meat." She hoped Adam didn't notice her uneasy glance at the forest behind them.

Fortunately, since she and Adam might be stuck here for a few days, she and Mike had packed more meals than they would usually carry because they wanted to take their time before a diminished larder forced them to divert to one of the scattered outposts of civilization along the coast to restock supplies. Both had mailed boxes filled with more homemade freeze-dried meals as well as candy bars, nuts, tea bags, toilet paper and more to Shearwater, where it would be held for pickup, a common arrangement for Inside Passage kayakers.

She found a chicken-with-wine-sauce entrée that she knew from experience was good, and brought two of the packets back to the "kitchen."

Adam watched her return with unnerving intensity and no real giveaway about his true thoughts. When she reached for a box of matches, he said, "Once you get that lit, we should talk."

"Now?"

"Why not?"

Because she didn't trust him? Hadn't decided yet what she should or shouldn't tell him? Good answers, but not ones she could share, so she only nodded.

BY THE TIME Claire put water on the stove and added the contents of both packets, she'd closed herself off. Adam could almost see her donning a mask. Not that he blamed her—she was too smart to have buried all doubts and bought into his claim to be a federal agent. That said, what was she hiding?

After setting clean dishes, forks and a big spoon within reach, she sat down. "I suppose we can't have a fire tonight."

"Not a chance."

"The gas tank for a motor that size must be small," she argued. "Even if they carry a couple of gas cans as backup, they'd be limited. Plus... would they keep searching after dark? That can be really dangerous. I mean, do they even have detailed charts for these islands?"

"The pilot was able to pinpoint where to meet up with the yacht. He insisted it had to be at high tide, and that they needed to bolt within an hour or two."

Claire looked dismayed. "I guess we can't rule it out, then."

"Them still prowling come twilight? No." He'd have to ask her if there were rocks hidden just beneath the surface that could split open the hull of a fragile dinghy. As for now...

She took a deep breath. "So. What are we going to talk about?"

"I need to know what electronic devices you have." Probably he sounded uncompromising. That's how he felt.

She blanked all emotion from her face and eyes, as if she'd had plenty of practice doing that. Why hadn't he asked what she did for a living? Could she possibly be a cop? She was tough enough.

"You think I'm hiding something so I can bring help you don't expect." She shook her head and rose to stir and check their dinner.

She didn't add, *Or is it help you don't want?* He heard her loud and clear anyway.

"I'm asking because we do need help." Right now, he was a very weak link. "We can't broadcast a general plea on the VHF radio, but we can make a call to someone who'll contact the Canadian Coast Guard for us."

"Well, here's the bad news. Because I apparently don't handle pressure well, the only device we have is my cell phone. Which might as well be a slab of marble right now."

She was lying. She had to be.

"You mentioned using the VHF to call for help."

"Before I remembered Mike had it today. We...sort of handed it back and forth." She closed her eyes. "I've read about how important it is to have multiple backups of anything important. I know better. I do."

"We have his kayak."

The open anguish that she let him see made him feel like a rat. "When I flipped it back over, the waterproof bag where he carried things he wanted within easy reach should have been in one of the mesh pockets just forward from the cockpit. My kayak has a day hatch, but it's the same concept. It's where we carry stuff like snacks, lip balm, suntan lotion…and emergency supplies and devices. He had a flare gun, too. He had to have lived long enough to grab that bag while he was freeing himself from the cockpit. Probably his last thought was to call for help."

"He wouldn't have had time," Adam said slowly.

"He…he never surfaced. The weird thing is that he also ripped off his PFD."

"Because it felt confining, or he thought he could swim underwater?" He shook his head. "A dying brain isn't rational."

"No." Claire bent her attention again to their meal, dishing up a portion into an aluminum bowl and handing it to him with a fork. She set the pan in front of her, apparently choosing not to dirty a second bowl, but didn't take a bite.

He waited a moment out of respect for her grief, but, damn, he was hungry, so finally he let himself start eating while keeping an eye on her. After a minute, she did the same.

They finished eating in silence. She sighed when she set the pan on a rock and leaned back again.

"We each carried a SPOT beacon. I don't know if you're familiar with them. They're what's called an emergency position indicator. You register it in your name, so if you have to push the button, the coast guard—or whoever—knows who they're supposed to rescue and, thanks to the GPS, where you are. You're only supposed to use it as a last resort." Claire paused. "Mike's would have been in that bag I told you about. I mean, I haven't searched, but that's where he always carried it except when we took a short hike or something like that."

Adam nodded.

"When…that guy shot Mike, I took out my SPOT, only I wasn't as careful as I should have been. I guess I was shocked, and I was wearing my gloves, and I think I didn't even look down. I was so transfixed by what was happening—"

"You dropped it. Overboard."

Shame burned on her cheeks. "They probably float, and eventually I looked for it, but not for very long. I didn't dare move, and I was watching you to see if there was any chance you were alive…"

"I understand," he made himself say, although their inability to summon help put them in more danger than she yet understood.

At last, her eyes met his. "I should have looked harder. It wasn't until I turned Mike's kayak over that I realized the bag was gone."

"I'd say we should have looked for anything that was floating when we went back to pick up the kayak, except..." He grimaced.

"You were in such bad shape. Getting you mostly out of the water wasn't enough to help, not when you were sopping wet and severely hypothermic. All I could think about was finding someplace to camp so I could get you warm."

"I thank you for your priorities." He'd have reached for her hand if he'd been close enough. "I thought I was dying."

"With water that might not even be fifty degrees, you would have died really quickly. Even so, if I'd taken just a few minutes longer—"

"What are the odds you'd have seen something as small as the SPOT? I'm assuming it's not a lot bigger than a cell phone."

"No."

"My philosophy is, what's done is done. It won't hurt to search everything your friend carried," Adam added, "just in case. We should probably inventory what he had anyway."

"He did carry an extra paddle, because the

one he was using was gone, too. You can tether them to the kayak, but…neither of us did that." More shame etched her voice.

He nodded matter-of-factly. Kicking herself now did neither of them any good. "Okay."

"If you're bored, he always brought a few books along." She wrinkled her nose. "Just what we need most. I have some, too. We'd swap sometimes, except we didn't share the same tastes."

Adam found a smile. "I'll check out the library. I'm thinking we almost have to stay put for a day or two."

Her eyebrows rose. "You actually think you can paddle that soon?"

"Do you have a better idea?" he asked dryly.

She was quiet.

Chapter Five

Fortunately, bright daylight kept them from needing flashlights or a kerosene light. Sunset wasn't until something like nine forty-five, although the color of the sky would deepen with twilight up to an hour before that. Unless she was imagining it, Claire felt the chill of the oncoming night, though. Frowning, she looked more closely at Adam.

Arms tightly crossed, he'd lost color in his face. Claire wished anew that they could afford to have a fire. She wondered if his core temperature had ever reached normal.

After she heated water for tea, he accepted the cup gratefully. While he drank his, she collected Mike's bags that held clothing and miscellaneous things and set them next to her chair. After taking a few swallows of her own sweetened tea, she pulled everything out of the first bag.

To inventory it, in Adamspeak.

"I shouldn't have let you put those wet boots

back on," she muttered. "I wish Mike's feet weren't so much smaller. Ah. His parka."

He looked up when she carried it to him. "You can tell I'm cold?"

Was there a faint slur in his words again? She was probably imagining it. "Of course I can."

He obediently held out his arm, but it quickly became apparent that they'd never get it on the injured arm. It was just plain too small to stretch across his broad back.

After a moment's thought, Claire fetched the sleeping bag that had been their top cover and brought it out as a replacement for the parka to wrap around Adam, creating a hood and making sure he could hold it closed with one hand. Then she tugged off the wet, cold boots and the fleece socks that had absorbed moisture.

"I think he has a second pair..." She went back to rooting through bags, finding what she sought and sliding them over Adam Taylor's feet. Then, with a sense of unreality, she sank back on her heels and assessed him. Here she was handling him as if she had a right to dress him and touch him as she pleased.

The circumstances that had made her so bold must feel as odd to him as they did to her.

I saved his life, she thought in astonishment. For all that she'd seriously practiced rescue techniques, she'd never imagined using them beyond helping someone back into a kayak after a failed roll.

He was watching her, even as she watched him. *Stranger. Remember?*

Right now, his eyes were deeply shadowed. The color was rich and bright, but changeable as the light and his mood shifted. They were beautiful eyes, set in a lean dark face. She was reassured, given her first sight of him, when she'd thought of his face as bone white. He was chilly, not freezing. Somehow, his brown stubble only emphasized the strength of his bone structure.

"You must have shaved this morning."

He lifted a hand from the sleeping bag as if to test his whisker growth but winced. "Damn shoulder."

"Normally I'd suggest icing it, but, well…"

"Yeah, no thanks."

Claire sighed. "I wish there were something we could *do*, instead of sitting here like, um…"

He lifted one eyebrow. "Sitting ducks?"

She made a face at him, almost hoping he'd smile.

He didn't. Instead, the lines in his face deepened, aging him. "I'd give a lot to be armed."

Guns made her uncomfortable. No one she knew well carried one, but she shared that wish anyway.

Whatever else she thought about this man,

she did believe he wouldn't hurt her. Steal all the paddles and leave her stranded, maybe—but he'd send help for her before he slid back into his sleazy underworld, wherever that was.

Fine, then.

"NORMALLY I GO to bed long before sunset, because getting on the water early is usually best. We don't have to plan for that, but even if we wanted to keep late hours, we have only a couple of flashlights and one kerosene lantern."

With quick alarm, Adam said, "We have to be careful not to show light."

"I kind of guessed you'd say that. Which is why I'm going to stow everything and then use the facilities."

Surprised, he glanced up at the sky, which seemed to have acquired a violet tint. "There's no indication it'll rain."

"You mean, why am I putting stuff away?" She was doing exactly that, starting with the clothes she'd pulled out of her partner's bags. "You'll totally understand if you once have raccoons visit during the night. They can do some damage, and make an awful mess."

He didn't think much about his childhood, but a memory came to him. "My—" Foster father. No, he had no desire to get into that. "We had raccoons knock over the garbage cans a few times."

"Bears can be just as bad. They're usually just curious, but they don't see any need to handle strange objects with delicacy."

Adam laughed, feeling better for it. On top of all his other reactions to this brave, capable woman, he was finding that he *liked* her. She made him laugh, and he hadn't done much of that in years.

"Anyway, we don't want to store food any closer to the tent than we have to. These bear vaults theoretically seal in the smell and can't be broken into, but I'd rather not have a bear trying to crack it open only a few feet from where I'm trapped in a sleeping bag."

Even as she talked, she put on a smaller quantity of water to heat and produced a small plastic bottle that must hold dish soap. A dish towel came from the same plastic ziplock bag. In minutes, she'd washed the few dishes and pan they'd used and stacked them efficiently into very little space.

He should offer to help, but felt very little inclination to move. He'd have to use the facilities, as she put it, but wasn't eager to stagger even ten feet deeper into the trees. Crawling into the tent was more appealing, except that he'd *really* hate having to get up in the middle of the night and drag himself outside to take a piss because he'd put it off.

"Here's a bag of Mike's toiletries," she said. "He might've brought a second toothbrush, but even if he didn't…"

Using a secondhand toothbrush wouldn't kill him, although it would feel wrong when the original owner hadn't been dead even a day. Still, Claire was probably hinting that she didn't want to share close quarters in the tent with someone who had bad breath.

"He did bring a shaver," she continued, "but usually only bothered to use it when we stopped somewhere with running water. *Hot* running water, and a shower. Partly because we carry our drinkable water, and it's wasteful to use it if we don't know when or where we can get more. And, in case you haven't noticed, this campsite has a tiny problem."

"No stream," he realized.

"Right."

"So plan to grow a beard."

She tipped her head to one side. "Have you ever had one?"

"A beard?" Adam was finding it harder to make out her face than it had been, which meant it must be getting on toward nine thirty. "Yeah, for the job." He hated even wearing stubble for more than a day or two; he always itched like crazy.

"If you'll excuse me." She had a roll of toilet paper in one hand, a plastic bag in the other. "I'll be back in a minute."

She seemed to disappear. Night had found them.

He hastily groped his way through the dead guy's toiletries, finding an unopened toothbrush, to his relief, and a small, half-used tube of toothpaste. Claire had left him a cup with less than an inch of water in it, which he made use of.

By the time she reappeared, he'd zipped the bag back up and given some thought to standing up.

"Let me help."

He flinched at the cold when she unwrapped him and tossed the sleeping bag into the tent before coming back to serve as a crutch. Once on his feet, he wavered for a moment, not liking his weakness and dangerous vulnerability. At the same time, he appreciated Claire's matter-of-fact brand of assistance.

Yeah, he liked her. He more than liked the feel of her curvy body pressed against his side. And then there was the fact that she was as strong as she was feminine.

He made himself say, "You can let go."

"You can make it by yourself?"

"Don't have to go far."

"Since you don't have shoes on, step carefully. Oh, um, do you need the toilet paper?"

He grinned at her delicate inquiry. "Not right now, thank you."

Of course, she was blushing.

What he wanted to know was whether she'd opt for her own sleeping bag tonight, or decide he still needed her body heat.

She waited for him to return from his little excursion, presumably so she could pick him up if he'd done a face-plant, but when he appeared, Claire slipped into the tent ahead of him.

Adam paused, first to listen for any indication other people were near—or even existed—and then to look up at the sky. Sailing the Pacific Coast, whatever his objective, he'd enjoyed standing out on deck and gazing up at the night sky. The splash of stars was astonishing, the faint glow of more distant ones visible in a way they never were in a good part of the lower forty-eight. Humanity had forgotten what they'd lost in their dependence on electricity.

Tonight, he needed to stretch out and not move for ten hours or so.

He lowered himself carefully to a crouch and then crawled into the small tent. A dark shape only, Claire reached out a hand to touch him.

"Are you warm enough? We can share a sleeping bag for the night if...you worry about holding on to your body heat."

She sounded endearingly shy, in contrast to her usual boldness.

Adam said, "I'd probably survive, but I'd prefer sharing."

Quiet for a moment, she said finally, "Okay, but only for warmth."

"I'll be good." He doubted he was in any physical shape to take his attraction to her anywhere.

"May I touch your forehead?"

Her hand still rested on his arm. He lifted it gently, uncurled her fingers and bent forward to give her access.

"You feel warm," she murmured.

"I did say—"

"I'm worrying that you might develop a fever."

"Oh." That made sense, except—"Wouldn't the salt water have cleaned out the wound adequately?"

"Probably. Never mind. I'm a worrier."

They were alike in that, then. Worrying, planning, staying wary, kept a man alive.

Sounding brisk, she suggested he remove a few layers of clothing, and offered to help when he needed it. He felt damn shaky by the time they were done, and he was able to lie down. Cold, too, but that was remedied when Claire climbed in with him and zipped up, closing out the night air.

Tonight, she'd even provided a pillow. He patted it, realizing it was one of those bags full of clothes.

She squirmed next to him, pulling up the second sleeping bag to provide additional warmth, then lay completely still. There couldn't be more than an inch separating them, given the tight quarters, but she was trying to stay separate.

He reached out his left arm in an invitation. "Isn't cuddling the idea?"

"I...guess so." She scooted closer.

Smiling at her stiff concession, Adam discovered that, while drowsiness was taking shape, he wasn't quite ready to sink into a deep slumber yet. Although Claire had laid her head on his good shoulder, she was far from relaxed.

"Will you tell me about yourself?" he asked to offer a distraction to the uncomfortable situation. "What do you do for a living?"

"I work in human resources. Not very exciting, I know." She told him the name of the good-sized manufacturing company. "I started at Boeing, worked for a hotel chain, then made this latest jump for a more senior position."

"How'd you get into that?"

"I majored in psychology. I couldn't really afford to go on for an advanced degree and wasn't sure I wanted to do counseling, so I looked out there to see what the degree was good for. What I learned in the psych classes actually does give me some insight I use for hiring and solving problems with existing employees."

"I bet." Adam thought about a couple of fellow agents who had major issues that most people shrugged off.

"What about you?"

Her breath whispered over the bare skin on his neck, momentarily sidetracking his brain.

"Chemistry. That's what I majored in. I went to work for the DEA as a chemist. The agency isn't all about illegal drugs. I got bored fast, and when I saw a chance to shift to becoming an agent, I jumped at it."

"Is it everything you thought it would be?"

Not a good time to confront his recent unease. "Sure. I liked action. I even liked playing roles. Did I mention that I acted regularly in theater productions during college?" Hoping she didn't notice his use of the past tense, he shut up.

"Undercover work must be hard on relationships," she observed thoughtfully.

Talking like this in the increasing darkness, unable to see expressions, was different.

"Yeah," he agreed. "I come back from being under for a couple of months, find friends have moved, fellow agents have been transferred. *I* get transferred." He frowned. "Fine by me. I'm a loner by nature."

Yet, he'd taken to wondering whether that was true. A lonely childhood had left him used to being alone, but did that mean it was his nature? Or had he just lost the chance to learn how to form or maintain lasting ties to anyone? All he felt was suspicion when he saw outwardly happy families.

Why the hell was he indulging in soul searching?

"Let's get to sleep," he said brusquely.

When she didn't say a word, Adam realized he wasn't quite ready to end the conversation.

"Are you involved with someone?" he heard himself ask.

"I thought you didn't want to talk anymore."

"Question just struck me." He hadn't wanted to lie, but he wasn't going to tell her that he'd been wondering from the moment he'd warmed up in her arms.

"I...was engaged," she said softly. "Broke it off about a year ago. Among other problems, he hated my kayaking. If he wasn't interested in a sport or hobby, *we* couldn't to do it."

He liked her wryness even as he suspected it hid lingering hurt. "Good thing you didn't go so far as marry the jackass."

Her chuckle raised goose bumps.

The small electrical charge blended with his increasing relaxation.

What kind of idiot would let her go? Adam didn't trust easily—or at all—but with this woman... He came suddenly alert. Sure, she'd surprised him. Astonished him, really, with her guts, strength and persistence, all in aid of a man she didn't even know. She'd never quit on someone she loved.

But she neither loved nor trusted him. And he shouldn't need the reminder. Speaking of idiots.

It was a long time until he surrendered to sleep, and she was still tense beside him when he checked out.

CLAIRE WAS FIRST aware of blissful warmth, then of a large hand wrapped around her side, securing her against a muscular body. His slow, deep breaths stirred her hair. She couldn't quite hear his heartbeats, but felt the rise and fall of his chest.

The stranger.

Abruptly awake, she realized how closely entwined they were. He'd stayed on his back, probably the only comfortable position for him given the shoulder injury. She'd flung one of her legs across his sometime during the night.

Time to retreat. She shouldn't have even offered to share a sleeping bag with him last night.

Then, the idea of holding each other felt comforting, even necessary. Now *dumb* was the word that came to mind.

She couldn't forget that she really didn't know him.

Chemistry major? Maybe. It's not like she could even ask casual questions to confirm he had basic knowledge. She'd hated the class in high school, and let any short-term knowledge go once she'd received a passing grade.

First, she very slowly lifted her leg off his, then squirmed backward. His arm tightened around her, but then relaxed and fell away. She saw no sign he was waking up. Unzipping the sleeping bag took some gymnastics, but she made her escape.

Morning or not, this wasn't sunbathing weather, so she dressed hastily and crawled out of the tent. One last peek found him still breathing deeply through parted lips. Definitely asleep.

They'd survived yesterday, but her nerves crawled at what today would bring.

Take advantage of the privacy for a quick trip to the woods, she decided, then a cup of coffee. When Adam appeared, she'd make breakfast, which usually consisted of oatmeal with dried fruit and sugar or honey.

Finish searching Mike's kayak. Who knew

what he might have stashed away? Pray she found his SPOT. He might have dropped it into a bag, comfortable with the knowledge that he had the VHF radio at hand, right?

Not convinced, Claire grabbed the toilet paper and made her absolutely necessary trip. Returning, she let herself enjoy the weak sun on her face.

The tide was on its way in. She ached to pack up and ready her kayak for departure. When the tide turned to go out again would be the perfect time to launch.

South to Haikai Passage would be the most direct way to find help, but they—she—would risk encountering the freighter. It had to be hovering at the first deep anchorage beyond the string of islands. But where?

Knowing how close Fitz Hugh Sound and the town of Namu were, as a crow flies, frustrated her. They wouldn't even have to reach the town, because they were certain to encounter heavy marine traffic on Fitz Hugh Sound, or before that when they got near a fishing camp. Getting there from here was the trick, though.

She continued to worry away at the problem.

West into Queen Charlotte Sound was too risky unless she left Adam behind. Dodging among islands had risks, too, but any weather change could mean swells or worse out on the open ocean. And, in her experience, the weather *would* change. There'd been more rainy or foggy days than sunny so far on this trip.

North seemed most logical, then, toward Hunter Channel and the Indigenous settlement of Bella Bella—assuming they didn't meet up with friendly fishermen or vacationers in a cabin cruiser on the way.

Maybe, given Adam's inexperience and injury, the best they could do for a day or two was sneak around islands and gain some distance from the searchers.

Unless she deserted Adam, they didn't dare go anywhere today, though. Tomorrow, however, they almost had to, because they'd run out of drinkable water.

She and Mike—

The stab of pain forced her to bend forward. It wasn't as if she hadn't thought about him, but now, everything she'd suppressed hit her. The first wrenching sob took her completely by surprise. She clapped her hand over her mouth to keep it silent, but nothing could stop the onslaught of grief that had chosen its time.

Chapter Six

Adam came awake with a rush, knowing instantly that something was missing.

Someone.

He surged to a sitting position, listening and not hearing a peep. As hyperalert as he always was, even in sleep he never let himself be unaware of any movement or sound from a woman in his bed, or men he bunked with. If Claire had decided she knew best and left, he'd—

Do what? he asked himself, angry. Dive into the freezing water and swim after her? That'd probably be faster than he'd move in a kayak, especially given the fierce pain in his right chest and back. At least the water would numb the pain if he dove in.

Swearing under his breath, he unzipped the bag and reached for the borrowed pants. For an almost-summer day, it was a lot colder than he liked. Not knowing the time increased his sense of being cut off from the world.

Dressed in the borrowed layers, he scrambled out, pulling the extra sleeping bag around him.

The minute he emerged from the tent, he saw her, sitting in her low-to-the-ground folding chair, nursing a hot cup of something in her hands. The relief was almost painful, although he noticed immediately that her eyes looked red and puffy.

She held a shushing finger to her lips, then pointed toward the trees. He went still, his gaze following hers.

A bald eagle sat on a branch not twenty-five feet from them. He clutched a fish in his talons, presumably breakfast. He also glared at them with savage disdain. They weren't supposed to be here.

"Friendly-looking guy," Adam murmured.

Claire smiled. "There's something almost reptilian in their eyes."

He'd seen bald eagles before; they were everywhere in western Washington, British Columbia and Alaska. Never this close, though. Never looked at one of the magnificent birds and known it was looking back.

After a moment, it spread broad wings and lifted off, fish still dangling, limp, from sharp talons.

Claire leaned forward to light the stove again. "Didn't want to have breakfast with us."

"Guess not."

"Coffee? Tea? Cocoa?"

He'd caught the fragrance of her roast. "Coffee."

First he made a detour, just as glad to have an excuse to gather himself before facing her scrutiny.

She averted her face when he returned and took his own seat. After a minute, he asked, "You okay?"

Claire lifted one shoulder in a tentative shrug. "Sure. It just hit me, that's all."

"Not helped by my presence, wearing your friend's clothes and using his toothbrush."

"No, that part doesn't bother me. I'm glad I could save someone. You know?"

He knew, although the ghosts of those he'd failed seemed more populous than the people he'd been able to pull out of bad situations. Still, he nodded.

"How do *you* feel?" she asked.

Now that the adrenaline was subsiding, he could evaluate his condition. "Better," he decided. "I felt steady walking. My brain isn't foggy."

"Good. You're due for some painkillers. After breakfast, let me take a look at your wounds."

He grimaced. "Do I have to take my shirt off?"

She laughed.

As she poured his coffee, he said, "The drug trade is thriving in the Caribbean, but it's warm there. I should have resisted the last transfer."

"But it's more beautiful here, right?"

He waggled a hand, and she laughed again.

He bet she'd enjoy kayaking in the vivid blue waters off Belize, say. He'd done some diving there, just for fun. *Fun* didn't play much part in his life, which might be why the memory was so vivid.

"You mind oatmeal?"

"As opposed to scrambled eggs and bacon?"

Nose wrinkled, she admitted, "Oats are all that's on the menu."

"I'll take it." Adam turned his gaze toward the water advancing between the sharp cut of rocks, white fingers reaching forward. Kelp had been deposited on the tiny pebble beach last night, but would likely be pulled out by the next low tide. As hidden as this spot was, the fact that Claire had found it was downright miraculous.

"Hear any motors this morning?"

"Nope. They could be circling different islands and still not be far away, though."

She declined his offer to help her clean up after breakfast, and he didn't blame her. She had it down to a fine art. Still, he watched carefully, not enjoying the experience of being a burden instead of useful.

Once Claire was done, she fetched the first-aid kit, and he reluctantly shed his sweatshirt. Her hands were gentle as she removed the wrappings and gauze. He could tell she was trying to be dispassionate, but this was nothing like an examination in a hospital or clinic. He was too aware of her, and her rising color betrayed equal consciousness of him even if she was careful not to meet his eyes.

Adam twisted his neck to see the bullet wound in front. He'd had them before, and this one looked clean to him. Claire seemed to agree, because all she did was apply more antibiotic ointment and cover it with gauze.

Once she'd moved behind him, she said, "This is going to leave a heck of a scar."

"Not my first one."

"No."

He didn't have a lot of sensation where he'd been slashed by a knife on his back, but he'd swear he felt her fingertips skim along the trajectory of the scar.

"Ever think you might be getting down to your last of nine lives?"

He'd never thought about it that way, but she might have a point.

Once she rewrapped him, he eased the sweatshirt back on.

Again, Claire didn't quite look at him as she retreated to her chair. Too much close contact?

"So." She sounded stiff. "I've been doing some thinking."

He waited.

"Mostly, about our route when we do make a move." Without waiting for a response, she laid out charts in front of him. Bending over, he studied them as she calmly told him her conclusions about their options.

He didn't disagree, although he said, "We're having a streak of good weather."

"Have you spent much time on this coast?"

"One previous trip in May on that rust bucket out of Juneau. Ended farther north than this, somewhere off the McNaughton islands. I can't claim to be an expert."

"Well, boaters in general check the weather every evening on the VHF radio, because it's so changeable. A large ship can handle a twenty-foot swell, but kayaks are relatively frail. You need to know whether it's safe to launch, given the route you plan for the day. It makes me nervous not having access to weather reports. A sunny sky when you launch at dawn doesn't mean it could be pouring rain four hours later, or high winds won't coincide with a rising tide. As it is…" She shrugged. "We'll have to judge from our limited viewpoint. In general, mornings are calm, but the winds rise in the afternoon. That's one reason we aim for early departures. Speaking of…"

He looked at her.

"Are the men looking for us likely to be out at dawn?"

Depended on how desperate they were getting, he thought. "If we can't paddle in the dark, as early as possible seems the safest to me."

She nodded. "Once the tide's all the way in, we'll have a lesson in kayaking. I can at least demonstrate some basics."

Paddling was not going to feel good. Adam had worked through pain before, but he was having too much time to anticipate the agony. Still, she was right. If nothing else, running out of drinking water would be a critical problem.

He traced the route she suggested with his finger. Convoluted, relatively speaking, but as long as they weren't spotted by his shipmates, they could escape the net they were trying to cast.

She slipped the charts back into the plastic that protected them from water damage, her gaze on him thoughtful.

Damn. She'd been working herself up to something. Adam tensed.

Her chin lifted. "I don't understand why they're so determined. They head back to Alaska, who can even prove they were ever here? I didn't see a name or registration number on the freighter, and I couldn't make out the name on the yacht. Plus, they didn't see me."

"You're hundred percent sure?"

Her forehead crinkled, but she said, "They wouldn't have left if they had."

"Look at it from their point of view. Say they didn't see you, but they decided to send someone back to make sure I was dead. What did they find? My body? Nope. The empty kayak, floating hull up? Not that, either. Maybe some debris, like the paddle, but probably not much, because the smaller stuff would have dispersed fast."

"Your body could have become submerged."

"But I was floating when they last saw me."

"And…and currents among these islands aren't as straightforward as the tide they deal with out on the open water."

"Kayak wasn't going to sink, though. And it's gaudy as hell."

Claire wanted to be stubborn, but her usually sky blue eyes had darkened with worry.

She went with stubborn. "They could be back in Juneau by now, but they're not. The drugs they transferred to the yacht are well on their way to a warehouse, ready for distribution. You're one man. You didn't have anything on you. No camera, no flash drive, no phone. Unless you have something stashed in Juneau, wherever you were staying, you can't prove anything. So why are they so worried?"

ADAM COULD WISH she weren't so logical, except she was his only backup. Reality was, the other agents involved in the overall investigation wouldn't start worrying about him for days, unless the freighter docked and he didn't check in. If that rusty old tub didn't reappear, they'd know he had no way to call, and would assume that something unexpected had come up and he was just keeping his head down. Doing his job.

That left Claire.

In a tight situation, he'd appreciate her brains as well as her astonishing strength. Right now, he wished she hadn't followed that train of logic quite so far down the line.

"I was there to nail them for drug trafficking. They've been transporting a steady stream of top-quality product to the US. I hadn't gotten even a hint of anything else, so no, I don't have anything useful stashed back in Juneau. I've passed on what I've learned." He paused. "I was back on board the ship when I overheard something not meant for my ears."

"Because your boss already distrusted you?"

"Because this wasn't something anyone high

up in the organization wanted the grunts to know. Most of us on that ship were grunts." He hesitated again, his instincts always to hold what he knew close. But he did need her, and if he had to scare her to make her more cautious, he'd do that. "This time," he said bluntly, "they'd been persuaded to carry something extra. I'm sure they were paid well, but it wouldn't surprise me if everyone who knew about the extra cargo isn't eliminated as soon as they show their faces back in Alaska."

"Weapons?" she whispered.

"Close enough."

Her eyes narrowed, and he caught himself twitching at her piercing scrutiny. She saw a lot deeper than he liked...or was damn good at faking it. He knew he wouldn't want to face her in a job interview if he were hiding part of his past.

Suddenly, she stood and crossed her arms, looking down at him. "Which makes it important you get the word out as soon as possible." Not a question.

He inclined his head in agreement.

"There wasn't anyone else on that ship or in port who can do that."

"No."

"Let me ask this."

He knew where she was going.

"What if they catch up with us and you get shot, but I make my getaway? What if I survive and you don't?" She bent toward him, with her slim body not as good at looming as she probably imagined, but she was making her point, all right. "Shouldn't I know who to contact and what to tell that person?"

Adam closed his eyes and scrubbed a hand through his hair, stiff from the salt water. "Yeah," he said hoarsely. This went against all his training, but she was right. Hell, he might die by making a beginner's mistake in the kayak she'd already described as frail. Or because he was injured, far from his peak health and strength.

"Well, then?"

He wanted to stand and pace. He needed to expend some of his fear. Aware of his weakness, he made himself stay put.

"Uranium. Terrorists convinced a couple of dumb-ass traffickers to carry the makings for a nuclear bomb—or several, who knows? All they saw was the bucks." He rubbed his thumb and forefingers together. "Worse thing is, I don't know what group is behind this, or who is waiting for the delivery." In his intensity, he leaned forward. "Passing on the name and registration number for the yacht is critical."

Claire stared at him, unblinking.

AFTER DROPPING HIS BOMBSHELL—bad pun—Adam made her memorize the information as well as the phone number to reach his boss.

Somehow, Claire stayed calm. Or managed to look calm anyway. She had a suspicion it would all hit her at some unexpected moment, just as grief for Mike had earlier. After everything she'd seen and learned in the past twenty-four hours, it took a lot to stir her out of her state of numbness.

Why was this happening to her? The biggest drama in her life had been the final months with Devin followed by their breakup. Right now, the Devin situation was receding fast in her rearview mirror. A jerk, so what. A real crisis? Terrorists getting their hands on the critical ingredient to manufacture a nuclear bomb... No comparison.

While brooding silently, she removed the evergreen branches hiding her kayak. Then she did her best to shove the huge, scary problems into a compartment in her brain that had a really sturdy door, focusing instead on carrying the kayak down to the water while slip-sliding on the rounded rocks that made up the beach. A careless trip could leave her injured, too.

Plus, it was easier to think about the next step than the big picture.

When Adam saw what she was doing, he

scowled and shot reflexively to his feet. "Let me help—"

"I carry it all the time. You don't need to be lifting anything yet."

His lips tightened and he relented. Claire had already noticed he didn't like to feel weaker than her. Of course, in his case, a need to be tough was probably a professional requirement.

He did watch in grim silence as she suited up, just in case she took a dunking. That got her thinking. Yes, he'd clearly hated letting her do the heavy work, but was that really because he needed to swagger in front of a woman? He'd been a lot more open to her suggestions and even orders than Devin ever would have been, even in a life-and-death situation. She'd like to think Adam just had old-fashioned good manners, or maybe tended to be protective. Being protective would come naturally to anyone in law enforcement, she assumed.

On the other hand, it was still open to question who he was. Maybe he'd cooked up this latest story to remove her doubts. It was certainly a good one. He'd hardly taken his eyes off her since his revelation about the contraband on the ship, as if he was assessing the effectiveness. Did she buy it? Didn't she?

Next step, she reminded herself.

"I'll help you pack and load your kayak tomorrow morning," she told him, "so we won't worry about any of that. Um…why don't you bring your chair down to the waterline instead of having to stand?"

She read a flicker in his eyes as frustration rather than annoyance at her continued coddling. Without a word, he picked up the lightweight chair and carried it down, picking his way carefully. His boots probably weren't entirely dry, but cold and clammy had to be an improvement on soggy. His own pants, sweater—with holes torn by the bullet front and back—socks and briefs were still draped over a huckleberry bush, probably dry.

Wow, would he be able to get into Mike's wet suit? Aghast, she wondered why she hadn't thought of this latest problem already. Damn.

Next step.

She shoved this new worry onto the pile.

Once she started her demonstration and found herself stumbling over her own tongue, Claire discovered how self-conscious Adam Taylor made her feel with his attention one hundred percent on her.

Of course, part of it was her awareness of his tall, strong body and what it looked like beneath his clothes. She knew the pattern of brown hair on his chest and had no trouble at all picturing his hard belly and strong thighs. She'd even saved a mental screenshot of him naked, despite pretending to herself that she wasn't looking.

By that time she had to be beet red, a step up from the sunburn she could never seem to avoid on these trips, given her extremely fair skin.

If Adam looked quizzical, who could blame him?

He watched intently as she showed him how to hold the superlight carbon fiber paddle. Mike had used a different style of paddle, so she used her own spare paddle for Adam to practice the grip.

She had him study the interior of the cockpit, with the seat and back cushions, the foam thigh braces and foot braces. The rudder... No, too much, she decided. It turned out he knew how to read the compass.

As she cinched up her spray skirt around her waist, Claire hoped Mike's wasn't too tight for Adam's more muscled torso. As a beginner, he was unlikely to do any rolling maneuvers, but without a spray skirt, even moderate waves would start filling the compartment with water. He'd be ankle deep or more in no time. Given the temperature of the water, he'd get cold. The risk would be even higher if he couldn't use the wet suit.

She stayed close, demonstrating forward and back strokes, the sweep stroke for turning, braces for stability. Then she returned to shore, pulled the kayak up and answered questions.

They ought to be holding this lesson in a swimming pool, or maybe a placid lake. She shouldn't be having to condense even basic techniques and knowledge into an hour exhibition. Even if he magically achieved mastery of the strokes, he'd still lack seamanship, the understanding of weather, tides, the subtle changes, what it took not to make a fatal mistake.

But finally, she said, "We need to figure out whether you can get into Mike's wet suit. As long as the weather stays nice, it's not as important—the fleece pants you're wearing will be okay. At least now you have some dry pants to change into at the end of the day. But there's no guarantee about weather, and if you get really wet it could trigger another bout with hypothermia."

He listened with an odd expression on his face. When she was finished, one side of his mouth turned up in a smile she could only think was tender. Her heart cramped hard.

"You're doing your best, you know," he said in his gravelly voice. "That's all you can do. Don't beat yourself up."

They stood close enough, she could have taken one step forward and leaned on him. Rested her forehead against his broad chest.

Even the temptation scared her. Instead, Claire snapped, "The better you plan, the more chance of success. You must know that."

"I do," he said quietly, that same quizzical look in his eyes, the same tilt to his mouth.

She turned her back to start to lift her kayak. Almost immediately, some of the weight vanished. Adam had grabbed the toggle at the stern with his left hand, and all she had to do was lift from the bow.

Weight shared.

Chapter Seven

Adam was all but twitching with his need to do *something*. Anything. Get on with tomorrow's plans, whether he was ready or not. Scramble through that damn tangle of vegetation to a point where he could watch surrounding waters through the binoculars while wishing they were a rifle scope.

Have sex.

That wasn't an option for a lot of reasons, starting with the fact that Claire Holland was a nice woman who'd risked her own life to save his. He'd known her for twenty-four hours—and that was generous, given that he'd been semiconscious for a good part of that time. There was plenty he still didn't know about her, but he'd bet she wasn't the kind of woman who had brief hookups with men, even if she felt the stirrings of attraction. So as fast as that ephemeral thought crossed his mind, he banished it.

He thought about suggesting they take the

kayaks out far enough to get a peek but knew that was not possible. He wouldn't be ready tomorrow, but he *really* wasn't ready right now.

The tentative warmth of the day felt good, if he'd been in the mood to lean back and relax.

Claire had picked up an electronic reader, told him that no, it wasn't displaying the time because it couldn't connect to the internet any more than her cell phone could. "I want to finish the book I'm reading," she'd announced, "and after that it'll be dead until I have a chance to charge it."

If she had a chance.

She had to be thinking that. He'd give anything to ensure she survived the coming days. Almost anything, Adam amended—he needed to get to someplace he could make a phone call. The bomb, depending on its size, could kill thousands to hundreds of thousands of people. That had to come first. Maybe it was fortunate that he needed *her* to get him to that phone. He wouldn't have to make a hard choice.

She abruptly set down her reader, stood and marched over to pick up a bag and carry it back to her chair. She dug inside and came up with a pile of tattered paperbacks that she held out to him.

"You're making me crazy. You can read, right?"

With all the hairs that had escaped the braid or broken off around her face, she made him think of a ruffled owl.

"You're peeling," he commented.

"Gee, I didn't notice." She waggled the books, and he accepted them.

Then she plunked down in her chair hard enough she was lucky not to bend the aluminum frame.

So, she didn't like him staring at her. He got that, but suspected she was as antsy as he was. They had the whole day to get through, and days were too damn long at this latitude. The two of them would have to go to bed well before the sun set if they were to make a really early start.

What in the hell were they supposed to *do* all day?

He bent his head to look at the book on top of the pile. A thriller, which wasn't likely to be pleasant recreational reading at the moment.

"Listen," Claire said suddenly.

Adam cocked his head. There it was, distant but audible. An outboard motor. That was no cabin cruiser or fishing boat.

His body went rigid.

Voice as tense as he felt, she said, "The tide's far enough out they can't get close enough to see us."

"I'm going out to where *I* can see them." He

rose to his feet. "Do you have flares, in case we get lucky and spot some innocent boaters?"

"Yes. Should we bring one?"

"Let's hold off. We don't dare set off a flare if there's any chance the skiff is nearby. Where are the binoculars?"

"You're not going without me," Claire insisted, just as she had yesterday.

She'd kept the binoculars close at hand. He was glad to have her given the difficulty of the trek. If he fell and did further damage to his shoulder, he was screwed. Likewise, if he sprained or broke an ankle or ribs. Or if she hurt herself. In fact, he had to grab her once when her boot became wedged under roots crisscrossing a crack between rocks, and she returned the favor a few minutes later.

The distant hum of the motor continued as background noise that rasped his nerve endings. If only he had a rifle.

No, better not to take a shot even if he'd had one. Unless he succeeded in killing both men in the boat, or punching enough holes in the aluminum hull to sink the thing, all he'd have done was pinpoint their current location.

Thinking about weapons gave him an idea, though. He'd check to see how many flares were available between the two kayaks. They could potentially be used as weapons, and he'd be especially happy to find a flare gun. In the event the two of them got cornered and were under attack, flares might draw attention his former buddies wouldn't like.

Today, Claire and he pushed farther out toward the rim of the island, although they paid the price of a sore ankle—in his case—and a wealth of scratches on both their faces and hands.

Once they had a good view, they hunkered down behind the scrappy vegetation and rounded granite.

After two or three minutes of waiting, Claire burst out, "It's like…the whine of black flies or mosquitoes!"

"I'd like to swat this one," he agreed.

The reflection off the water was bright enough, he had to blink frequently. "Did Mike have dark glasses?" he asked.

She gave him a startled glance. "Yes. Unless they were in—" Her voice became smaller. "I think he might have been wearing them."

Oh, well. Protection for his eyes would be a luxury, not an essential.

Once again, she spotted the boat before he did, making him think she had exceptionally sharp eyes. "There. Only…it's not the same boat."

He trained the binoculars on the gray-green inflatable boat, and immediately confirmed the identities of the two men in it. "Son of a—" he muttered under his breath. "The skiff ran really low in the water with both of them aboard. This is newer and larger." Motor didn't sound any more powerful, though.

"Do you suppose they have a map showing potential campsites?" Claire asked.

He took his eyes off the boat. "I don't know. Do you?"

"Yes. I've been worrying that the campsites everyone knows about might not be safe for us."

Adam handed her the binoculars. If she ended up alone, she had to know the bad guys when she saw them. "Take a look. Memorize their faces."

She didn't look happy about the directive, but adjusted the binoculars and stared through them for a long minute.

"Those campsites," Adam said. "Who is likely to stay at them?"

Lowering the binoculars, she answered, "Other kayakers, mostly."

"Who'd be carrying a VHF radio or satellite tracker."

"Yes, but…"

He kept an eye on the inflatable, which was gradually growing closer, but also watched her.

"Well, would help come fast enough if *they* see us? And…would we be endangering other people?"

Given a new worry, he quit listening and took

back the binoculars. Unless the path of the boat changed, the two men wouldn't be able to miss seeing the almost-hidden entrance through the crack in the sculpted rock wall of the island. All they'd have to do was come back once the tide was high again.

Adam and Claire wouldn't have any defense against being strafed with bullets from semiautomatic weapons.

LUNCH CONSISTED OF rehydrated soup, dried fruit and a candy bar each.

Adam was never chatty, and Claire had been so frightened by the near disaster that she still felt shaky.

Something had distracted those men. The one sitting in the bow had pointed northeast, and the pilot had steered them into a curve leading away from Adam's and her hideout.

Thank God.

Adam had kept a sharp eye on her for a while, but finally started reading one of the books from the pile. He'd tossed aside a couple of them— Mike had really liked thrillers—in favor of an older science fiction novel, *The Mote in God's Eye*, that even Claire had read and enjoyed once upon a time, although she didn't remember much about it. Even as he appeared to be engrossed in the story, she suspected his attention was as divided as hers was.

She'd let herself feel almost safe here. Illusion obliterated, she started at every tiny sound, from a flurry of wings as a flock of ravens came to rest in the taller trees behind her, to the cries of gulls and terns. The ravens especially disturbed her. Northwest Coast First Nations legend had it that ravens perching on a house meant a death would come.

Once they heard a powerful marine engine, but too far in the distance. If anyone on board saw a flare, they'd come looking, but as Adam had pointed out, someone closer could find them first.

At a loud splash, she must have jumped a foot, but the new arrival was a black oystercatcher, a foot-and-a-half-tall bird with distinctive red markings that paddled into sight and, ignoring them, poked in the tidal pools to one side of their miniature beach.

If a black bear had waddled into sight, Claire probably would have had a heart attack.

"I doubt they'll be back today." Adam didn't even look up from his book, but he'd read her anxiety just fine.

"I know."

His faint smile annoyed her.

She stared at the lit screen of her electronic

reader and discovered she was on the last page of the book. She hadn't a clue what had happened in the previous two chapters and didn't care. Only a sliver of battery life remained. She closed the cover but still clutched the reader in a tight grip. She could grab her remaining paperback, or sort through Mike's, but reading was futile.

With the bad guys apparently gone for now, maybe she and Adam should pack up and make a run for it. Claire almost opened her mouth to suggest it, but then she took a good look at his face.

The flesh seemed to have evaporated, leaving skin stretched tight from sharp cheekbones to the bony line of his jaw. If anything, the stubble enhanced the gaunt effect. Creases marred his forehead, and his eyes… She waited for him to lift his head.

When he did, she sucked in a breath. "You hurt."

"Nothing I can't handle," he said shortly.

"Why would you suffer when you don't have to?" She gave her head an exasperated shake. "You've been wounded before. Surely a few doctors along the way have given you the lecture about the benefits of staying on top of the pain?" Her voice had been steadily rising. "As in, you'll heal faster?"

"I did intend to ask for some more Tylenol," he admitted.

"I think you should go for the heavy-duty stuff. Maybe even take a nap." Except she'd be left alone out here, afraid to miss a single sound.

"No nap. I'll take the meds, though."

So he hurt even more than she'd guessed. Shaking her head, Claire poured water into a cup and handed it to him with two of the pills. He gulped them down and gave her back the cup.

"I don't like admitting to weaknesses," he said after a minute.

An apology, she suspected.

"It's not a weakness to feel the normal symptoms from a wound. I mean, a bullet went *through* you."

"Yeah. I've had a lot of practice at hiding what I'm feeling."

"Because of your job?"

He rubbed his hand through his hair, which had to be stiff with dried salt. She kept watching him, and finally he said, "I'm guessing you grew up feeling secure."

"I did. My parents split up when I was fourteen, but...yeah. I knew Mom and I'd be staying in the house. I'd keep going to the same school. It was just weird with Dad not there. I was ashamed for friends to find out."

"Did he stay in touch?"

"Sure. He didn't always show up when he'd promised to, but he mostly paid the child support, and my mother encouraged me to understand he was having a hard time."

"In what way?"

None of this was his business, but he was a good listener, and they had to do *something* while they waited for nightfall.

"He was drinking heavily. After a couple of DUIs, he spent months in jail. It took him a couple of years to get himself together, but too late for Mom."

"He'd broken her trust."

"I guess so." He'd broken hers, too, but he stayed sober the days he took her out for lunch or to do something fun, like ride the ferry or go to the Puyallup Fair, so she'd been able to continue loving him, and knew he loved her. Still, she'd felt abandoned, which might explain why she'd stubbornly stayed with Devin despite all the warning signs.

What an unexpected conversation.

"Did your father walk out on you and your mom?"

"Before I was born." Long pause. "My mother had her own problems. She worked as a waitress or in a bar, from what I remember. I was four when she didn't pick me up at this home day care. I went into the system. Never saw her again."

"That's awful." Claire knew she couldn't let him think she felt pity. He'd close up tight. Tighter than he already was, that is. He was talking, but not giving away much emotion. "Did she... Were her problems with drugs?"

Their eyes met, and he made a rough sound. "Guess I'm obvious. Yeah, I have a few memories of watching her shooting up. When she couldn't afford her next hit—" He shook his head.

Claire didn't even like to think about what he hadn't said.

"Did you look for either of your parents later?"

"Mother. Found out she'd died a couple of years later. My father...no. Why would I?"

She understood. She wouldn't have, either.

He stayed quiet for what had to be several minutes, not reading, just frowning. At last he shook himself. "I don't usually talk about my past."

"We're spending a lot of time together." No TV, tablets or phones to distract them. And... she had shared more than she'd have expected with him, too.

Adam grunted what could have been a laugh.

"Sunbathing and dining together. You've started introducing me to your favorite sport."

Sleeping together, too, she couldn't help thinking.

"Right." She smiled. "Nothing but fun."

"Might be, under other circumstances."

The painkillers must be having an effect, because Adam's eyelids grew heavy. He lapsed into silence for a few minutes again, Claire not breaking it. A raven cawed and, to her relief, they all took wing. Spreading their blessings elsewhere? Adam's gaze appeared unfocused. He really should take a nap.

His voice startled her. "Look."

"What?" She tipped her head back to see the sky, the endless blue marked by a long vapor trail. Claire felt a strange pang. There was proof they weren't alone in the world, but they might as well be.

"You like your job?" Adam asked unexpectedly.

Still gazing at the vapor trail, she had to think about that. "Most of the time, but…it's a job, not a passion. You know. I suppose I wouldn't miss it, but I'm satisfied. I make a good living, and I can put it out of my mind when I leave the office." She realized how that sounded. "I guess you can't do the same, can you?"

"Ya think?"

"I don't think I'd enjoy a job where I got *shot* on an average day in the office," she said honestly.

That earned her one of his hoarse laughs. "Yesterday wasn't an average day."

"You have an awful lot of scars."

"Yeah." He fell back to brooding.

It was all she could do not to fiddle, or chatter brightly about some inane topic. Desperate at last, she said, "Would you like some hot chocolate? Or coffee? Or…"

His eyes, now bloodshot, met hers. "Can we spare the water?"

"We can't let ourselves get dehydrated."

"Hot chocolate."

Heating the water and preparing the drinks kept her busy for a few minutes. Once she handed over his, she worried when she saw the way he cradled the mug and breathed in the steam. She certainly hadn't stripped to her T-shirt, but the day wasn't *cold*. If he started to shiver…

But he took a sip and lifted his head to study her. "Why'd you break up with the fiancé?"

Nosy, but she'd been dying to ask if he'd been—or was currently—married or living with someone.

Anyway, why not answer? Once they reached

safety, she doubted she and Adam would ever see each other again.

"He didn't like being challenged, not even in little ways. If he told me his opinion about some issue and I mentioned an article I'd read that included facts that didn't support what he was saying, he'd be cutting. He'd say I was credulous, believing everything I read no matter what the source. He hated that I made more money than he did. It got so he was constantly putting me down, both in private and in front of our friends. He seemed so confident when we first met." Claire felt her face twist. "Maybe I'm a know-it-all—"

Adam made a derisive sound. "Sounds like he wanted a submissive partner whose goal in life was to make him feel big." His eyes narrowed. "Did he get abusive?"

"You mean, did he hit me?" She clenched her jaw. It was an effort to say the rest. "Yes. Once. That was the end."

"Did he grovel afterward and tell you he wouldn't do anything like that again?"

She nodded. "I told him he needed counseling, went to spend the night at a friend's house—" Mike and Shelby's, of course "—and told Devin to be out by the time I got home from work the next day."

"Your place? Bet that rubbed him the wrong way."

Of course it had, but he liked living above his income. "He had an apartment—I own a nice condo."

She hadn't been surprised to come home to find him still there. He'd packed, but he had also cooked a fancy dinner and set a candlelit table. He'd uncorked a bottle of wine to breathe.

Fortunately, she'd had the forethought to ask Mike to go with her. Devin screamed ugly accusations and obscenities at her as he handed over his key and left.

After she was done crying, she and Mike had planned this trip but had to wait until they'd both saved enough vacation from their jobs to take it.

He'd given her the gift of anticipation, even hope, and what had his kindness and friendship given him? A senseless death.

She started to cry and had to cover her face with her hands to try to hide it. The next thing she knew, Adam was kneeling by her chair and embracing her. She let herself cry against his shoulder for a minute, that was all, then lifted her head to give him a shaky smile and to lay her hand lightly over his heart.

"Thanks."

"That son of a bitch."

Surprised, she said, "I wasn't crying about Devin. It was…"

She didn't have to explain, it was for Mike… and Shelby. He retreated to his chair and stayed silent for so long.

"Are you married?"

His head turned sharply. "God, no!"

Well, that was telling her. Not that she was foolish enough to be thinking of him in that context.

"Not a fan of the institution?" she asked.

"It's not that." He frowned. "I don't know many people who've made a success of marriage, though."

"You don't run in the best circles," she pointed out.

Adam shrugged a concession. "I know agents who've been divorced two or even three times. There's a flaw in the 'absence makes the heart grow fonder' theory."

"It would be hard. But if you love someone enough, and that person loves what they are doing…"

"Nice idea, but then you have children, and you're trying to be both parents, hold down a job, make decisions you resent having to make on your own, while they are off doing God knows what, and what if your partner is having an affair while away from home? Or what if they come home with yet another bullet hole?"

"You can't tell me there aren't spouses tough enough to take it."

His eyes, unblinking, held hers longer than was comfortable. Then he growled, "Let's talk about something else."

And what exactly would that be?

Chapter Eight

Bedtime rolled around at last, thank God. Adam swore he wouldn't ask Claire to share the sleeping bag with him, but, damn, he wanted to. Her curves fit him just right. She didn't have to worry that he'd expect anything but a warm body to hold. He'd been deluded earlier, thinking about having sex.

"Strange trying to sleep when the sun is still high," he grumbled, crawling first into the tent. It was dim inside here, but far from dark.

"Didn't you on that boat?"

"We had bunks inside."

"Oh. Well, if it really bothers you, I can throw a space blanket over the tent. That would help."

"I'll be fine." Especially if he could clutch her to him like a gently worn teddy bear—or the lover he'd like her to be, when he regained his strength. When they were both safe.

"Okay."

He couldn't quite see what she was doing, but

thought when her head turned that she was taking a last scan to be sure everything was securely stowed. Then she crawled in, too, and let the flaps fall closed.

"You never zip those," he commented.

"Huh? Oh. I like to be able to see what's coming without fumbling for the zipper."

There was a thought.

He'd taken some more of the hard-hitting painkillers in hopes they'd give him both a good night's sleep and a boost in healing. They hadn't quite taken effect yet, though, so he groaned and swore a couple of times while inserting himself in the sleeping bag.

He closed his eyes as she stripped off most of her clothes, although he heard the rustles and sighs just fine. Pain or not, his body was responding to the images that filled his head.

"Let me feel your forehead," she said softly. A moment later, her palm settled on his brow. "No fever." She sounded as if she was talking to herself.

He lay tense, wishing he could think of a good excuse to ask her to join him.

"I suppose I should, um, sleep in my own bag tonight. In Mike's actually, since you're in mine, but—" Sounding flustered, she broke off.

"Either way is fine." He made sure she could

tell he was okay either way. "But I liked sleeping with you."

After a very long pause, she said, "I liked sleeping with you, too. It was…comforting."

He didn't say anything.

"Why not?" she decided, and a moment later she squirmed her way in with him, tugged up the zipper, shook out the second sleeping bag into a cozy layer and unerringly found the hollow below his shoulder to pillow her head.

He tugged her closer, wrapped his arm around her and smiled up at the peaked roof of the tent. Now he was too relaxed to waste the energy thinking about morning, and the risky run from danger.

CLAIRE FLOATED TEN or fifteen feet off to Adam's left, looking as if she and the kayak were one. He felt as awkward as a big man perched in a first grader's chair, pretending he was comfortable. His knees weren't quite up to his nose, but that was only because they were trapped beneath the deck of the kayak.

Didn't help that he was humiliatingly aware that he required frequent critiquing.

"You're trying to do it all with your arms," she said just then. "Use your torso." She demonstrated a stroke that had her upper body twisting side to side as she paddled. Her kayak shot ahead as if a flick of a fishtail propelled it.

He tried what she suggested and found she was right—this was easier and put slightly less strain on his painful right upper quadrant. Which wasn't saying much.

The sky had still been pearly when they left their campsite, having to carry the kayaks over the long, narrow stretch of smooth, slimy cobblestones bared after the tide went out, but once afloat they emerged from between the wave-sculpted cliffs to find themselves alone. Or so it seemed. With the multitude of islands and rocky islets topped by wind-twisted trees, another boat could be hiding just out of sight, as Claire had been when her partner was shot. She'd been right that the air was still, the morning utterly quiet. Eerie wisps of fog hovered, not quite touching the water nor reaching as high as the trees. From time to time, she'd become oddly indistinct, until he reached the same band of fog and then glided through it.

They had chosen the northerly route, winding between islands, planning to hug the east coast of Spider Island. There were a couple of designated campsites there. He'd argued they circle to the west side of the biggest island in this immediate area because he feared Spider

Channel would be too open, exposing them to watching eyes.

Claire had nixed that, pointing out that in the channel, they would be sheltered. On the west coast they'd be exposed to open ocean with powerful tidal currents and swells that could reach ten feet high even if the weather remained fair.

"You're a raw beginner," she reminded him, as if he'd forgotten, "and injured besides. I hate the idea of us losing sight of each other even briefly as we dip between swells and climb over them."

"You're the expert," he had said simply.

Now as they glided past yet another island, Claire suddenly back paddled and said sharply, "Look!"

The pain already crippling Adam more than he'd anticipated; he was grateful to let his paddle rest across the cockpit while he squinted to see what she had.

That didn't take much effort, since the bright red kayak stood out in this blue-and-green-and-pale-gray landscape. Hope of finding a fellow traveler who had a radio or SPOT didn't even have a chance to catch hold, because it was immediately obvious that there was no paddler.

"Somebody may be in the water!" she cried and shot forward at a speed he couldn't equal.

"Claire!"

But if she heard him, she didn't stop.

He dug in to catch her, but his kayak immediately felt unstable, the rocking making him afraid he might capsize. And he was no longer going straight after her, either; clearly, he was favoring his right arm. Adam made himself slow down and regain the steady pace he'd so far maintained.

For the, what, fifteen minutes they'd been on the water?

He didn't hear the sound of any engine. Trouble was only this single kayak, bobbing on the lift of the waves.

Claire reached it well before he did, and immediately began to cast in increasing circles around it. He glided up to the empty kayak and back paddled until he could lay a hand on it.

Half expecting to see streaks of blood or bullet holes in the hull, he found nothing alarming—except for the missing kayaker.

Claire came back to join him. "It might have floated out of reach when someone was launching, or if they didn't tie it up last night." The anxiety in her eyes told him she didn't believe her own explanation.

"From where?" he asked.

She looked around. "There's a picnic spot, maybe good for emergency camping, not far from here. Let's check there."

She gave him a comprehensive look that probably saw through his stoic veneer.

He said, "Why don't we look in the day hatch first?"

"You're right." She snapped it open, and he saw a water bottle, snacks, lip ointment, suntan lotion, a flare and some other miscellaneous items. Claire lifted a broad-brimmed foldable hat. "A cell phone."

They hovered over it from opposite sides of the empty kayak. Unsurprisingly, its charge was either gone or it could only be activated by a fingerprint.

"Damn," he muttered. "Wouldn't anyone kayaking out here have at least a VHF radio?"

"Yes, but he might have it in the vest pocket." She patted hers. "I carried the SPOT in there."

Frustrated, Adam watched as Claire snapped a towline on a loop at the bow and started paddling. She'd only left a short line, and Adam followed like a duckling.

He didn't like this. The empty kayak wasn't quite the same color as the one he was paddling, nor the same shape—it was shorter by a couple of feet, too—but it *was* red. Would Dwayne and the others have noticed the orange shading into red on this one? It wouldn't have been until later that they started worrying about the combined absence of his body and the kayak.

No, he seriously doubted they'd have paid attention to any subtleties.

Claire had them circling an island with the ocean-hewn rock walls washed pale and oddly smooth in a way that was typical. She was moving faster than she had earlier, driven to find the missing person. Adam labored to keep up.

An inlet opened, and he groaned in relief, knowing she wouldn't hear him.

He heard her half-whimpered "Oh, God," followed by a tremulous, "Mike?"

Within moments, he came abreast of her and saw the body bumping against the rocks.

He had no idea what her friend had worn when he was shot, but knew he'd shed his yellow flotation vest. This body still wore his.

"It can't be Mike," he said flatly. "Let me closer."

Sunburned or no, her face had blanched. She did something complicated with her paddle that enabled her to edge out of the way. The empty kayak bumped against Adam's and almost forced him into the wall, but he pushed away with his paddle. When he reached the body, he snagged it by the vest.

"Watch out!"

Hell. He'd almost gone over. "Help me get him across my deck."

She scooted over so that she could stabilize

his kayak with their paddles lying across both decks as he bent over again. A man's weight coupled with the soaking-wet garments was almost too much for his one-handed grip, but he forced himself to use his right hand, too, and heaved upward.

He didn't see the face, but with the body draped right in front of him he couldn't miss the several holes left by bullets punching through the puffy yellow PFD.

Claire's shocked stare told him she understood what had happened to this poor bastard—and why it had happened.

THEY DIDN'T HAVE a lot of choice but to land on the small, gravel beach.

Claire released herself from her cockpit and then her spray skirt before pulling her own kayak a few feet higher on the beach and reeling in the towline so she could capture the empty kayak.

"Do we dare stay here even for a little while?" she asked. They hadn't made half a mile yet.

But then she saw Adam's face as he stumbled climbing out of his own kayak. His face looked almost as bad as it had when she saw him surface after he'd been shot. White lines of pain bracketed his mouth.

"You hurt yourself pulling the body on board."

He glanced up. "No. Already hurt. Damn. Help me get this guy up to dry ground."

"Yes. Okay." She had to swallow some bile as she looked at the body sprawled over Adam's kayak. This wasn't Mike; she knew it wasn't, but…his body would look as bad.

Worse, she thought, after being in the water for two extra days.

Adam mumbled something profane as he looked around them. Then he scrubbed a hand over his face. "Can you tell if he camped here last night?"

"Let me look."

It didn't take her long to find a rectangle of flattened vegetation where a tent must have been pitched—although it wouldn't have been comfortable to sleep in, given the ridge of a tree root that ran the length of it—and some scuffed moss.

"Somebody did," she said. A furrow in the gravel added to the tale. "One kayak."

"Okay. I have to think. While I do that, let's search the kayak and the body for anything useful."

"Why don't we both think?" she suggested a little tartly, despite the horror she had trouble moving past.

He grimaced. "Right. I didn't mean to imply— Sorry. I'm just used to being on my own. What we need to decide is what to do with the body and the kayak, and whether we'd be safer hunkering down here for the night or going on."

She came close to shouldering him out of the way so she could take most of the weight, but needed Adam's strength. Now she knew where the term *deadweight* came from. The body flopped onto the beach, the head coming to rest so that the man stared up at the blue sky.

Having gotten to know a lot of people in the Seattle area who were into sea kayaking, she'd been afraid she might recognize the victim, but he was a stranger. His brown hair was mostly contained in a short ponytail. Otherwise, he had brown eyes and a stubbled jaw and was a big guy.

She and Adam wrestled the PFD off the body, but found the pocket empty. A pat down came up empty.

The two of them divided up the hatches on the kayak for a thorough hunt for identification, a SPOT or VHF radio and food, water and clothes that might fit Adam. She hated the idea of stripping the wet suit from the victim, but knew she'd have to. Adam might need it. He hadn't been able to squeeze into Mike's. If they hit rough or substantially colder weather, it would be critical.

"This'll solve one of our problems," Adam said after a minute.

She took a step to peek into the hatch right

behind the cockpit, seeing three bags of drinking water. One ten-liter, two six.

"Yes." She gestured at the open deck hatch. "I took another look in here, but unless you like his brand of suntan lotion better than what Mike and I were carrying, there's nothing useful."

Adam's mouth tightened. "I'd hoped those SOBs might have been careless."

Claire didn't say anything.

She found two bags filled with clothing and set them aside. From the clanking sound behind her, she could tell Adam was digging through a bag with dishes and pans.

"Keep an eye out for any extra fuel canisters for the stove," she said over her shoulder.

"What about the food?"

"I don't know. Let me look at it while you go through these clothes."

Adam's expression was almost as grim as she felt when they changed places.

She saw right away that he'd set aside a knife with a six-inch blade. She had one, too, but the more the merrier, right? She guessed that depended on perspective. Adam's main goal in this search had probably been weapons. He'd found a flare gun, too, although she wasn't sure that qualified as a weapon, despite appearances.

Most of the contents of the bag holding kitchen gear were duplicates of things she and Mike had carried. She repacked it with unnecessary care, then evaluated the foodstuffs, deciding on some that would supplement what they already had.

Adam straightened, although he was still kneeling. "Here's a small bag that has...a wallet." One by one, he set items aside. "Canadian passport, wristwatch, sunglasses."

A lump formed in her throat. "What's his name?" Her gaze was drawn to the body.

"Kyle Sheppard." Adam sounded completely unemotional. "Twenty-eight years old. He's from Winnipeg."

Only twenty-eight. Claire shivered, unable to take her eyes off the young man's face. "Lots of lakes there. That's probably where he started kayaking."

When she finally glanced at Adam, she saw him rifling through the contents of the wallet.

"Credit cards, Canadian money, phone card, what looks like a car key," he said after a minute. "And a photo."

She didn't ask; she couldn't.

Adam rolled his shoulders and closed the wallet, dropped it on the small pile, then went back to his task of digging through the bag.

Claire returned each dry bag to one hatch after another once she'd looked through it. They almost had to put the kayak back into the water, and wouldn't want a cursory inspection to reveal that the contents had been searched.

Adam salvaged a fair pile of clothes. Without consulting her, he pulled bags from his kayak and pulled out Mike's clothes that didn't fit him, filling the bags with this new stuff that did. He even sat down and tried on a pair of sturdy sandals before adding them to the "keep" pile.

Claire spoke up. "When you're done, I'll tow the kayak out a little ways and turn it loose again."

He frowned at her. "You won't go far?"

"I won't need to. With the tide going out, it'll carry the kayak away."

He nodded. "Next question is, should we stay here under the assumption they've already been and have no reason to come back?"

"We haven't come very far this morning—" To put it mildly. "I'm thinking we're a couple of hours paddling away from the campsite I had in mind."

Adam didn't noticeably react. Finally, he said, "I can make it if I have to."

All she had to do was remember the expression on his face when they first landed to know how much he'd suffer if they went on. They'd been too optimistic—or was *desperate* a better word?—in thinking Adam would be ready to paddle a kayak so soon, after such a serious injury. Would another night's rest give him enough chance to heal to make a difference?

Tomorrow would have to be better than today. Only…

She had to say this. "The body will attract any wildlife on the island."

"Oh, hell."

The idea of putting the body—no, a dead young man named Kyle Sheppard—back into the water at the mercy of the tides and sea life horrified her. How would they be able to tell Kyle's family what they'd done? She hadn't been able to recover Mike's body, and that would haunt her. But this…

With short, angry movements, Adam restuffed the bags he'd had open and carried them to the kayak. "Let's start by getting rid of this," he said.

Feeling sick at their choices, Claire nodded.

Chapter Nine

Having Claire even momentarily out of his sight didn't sit well with Adam. He should have used the time to strip the body of the wet suit he knew he needed, but that would have taken concentration he couldn't summon. Instead, despite the pain ripping through his shoulder, chest and arm and the weakness that had taken him so aback once they launched this morning, he paced the width of the beach repeatedly, tripping twice because his eyes were trained on the water rather than the ground in front of him.

He hated knowing *he* was the one holding them up, endangering her because he was incapable of completing a distance on the water that a kid probably could.

When she reappeared, gliding toward shore, he wanted to yell at her for taking too long—but when he glanced at the wristwatch he'd appropriated it was to see that only fifteen minutes had passed.

Claire climbed out of her kayak and began pulling it ashore. Her eyes met his then shied away. Yeah, he hadn't hidden his emotions as well as he'd have liked.

"I had an idea," she said hesitantly. "If you think staying here is a good idea."

"What's that?"

"We could weigh his body down in the water someplace accessible, then recover it in the morning and, I don't know, hang it over a tree limb or something like that. I can mark this beach on my chart so rescuers will know where to come for him."

Adam's relief surprised him. He didn't need to point out that they had no way of guaranteeing that something wouldn't get to the body in the water, weighed down or no, but it was a more palatable solution than just dumping it. He'd been bothered by the photo in the wallet of a nice older couple with warm smiles. A young guy like Kyle Sheppard probably kept most photographs on his phone, but he'd carried a printed one, too. His parents meant a whole lot to him. Adam knew he'd gotten hardened, to an extent, and since he lacked family, a wife, even a girlfriend, he could have lived knowing the guy's body would never be found to hand over to family. But that would be harder for Claire, and even he… Hell. Maybe it was knowing her that made him squeamish.

"Let's do that," he agreed. "Although I'd like to get our camp and kayaks out of sight from the water if we possibly can. What if we don't set up a tent?"

"That'd be fine unless the weather turns this afternoon. Or if we get swarmed by mosquitoes or flies. Let's hold off and see."

They hauled the kayaks up and unloaded what they expected to need, Claire doing more of the work than Adam liked, then got them out of sight behind dense evergreen branches. Neither said a word as they took the wet suit, gloves and neoprene booties off the body before looking around for suitable rocks to weigh down the cadaver.

The tide had withdrawn to reveal a pool that was deep enough for their purposes. Recovering the body in the morning, with the higher tide, would be more of a challenge.

Back to where the wet suit lay on the gravel, Claire said, "Let's rinse this out," and began methodically to turn it inside out and dip it in the water. Adam hadn't loved the idea of donning garments taken right off a dead guy, especially ones that couldn't be aired out like those made of breathable fabric.

Lucky the sun still shone today, giving the suit time to dry out.

He'd gotten his boots and the calves of his cargo pants wet, so he blanked out the source of his new wardrobe and changed into a pair of similar chinos that were only a little tight in the waist—Kyle had been thinner than Adam—and into dry socks and the sandals.

Claire pushed aside branches and found a wide enough spot beneath the dense canopy to lay out their sleeping bags, the tent pieces beside them, the camp stove just a few feet away.

"I'm going to heat some of this extra water and give myself a sponge bath," she announced.

Adam was startled by the sound of her voice, only then realizing how little she'd spoken after they made the important decisions. Of course, he immediately got to thinking about her peeling off clothes and washing. Probably she just wanted to be clean, but she'd also been handling a corpse. Yeah, she might be hoping soap and water could scrub away that experience.

It wouldn't, but she'd find that out soon enough.

"I wouldn't mind doing the same," he admitted. After the past few days, and especially today, he wasn't likely to smell very good.

Once the first water had warmed, Claire produced a skimpy towel, a washcloth and soap, collected a clean set of clothes and disappeared behind a sizable tree trunk. He sat down with his back to her, but he heard her garments dropping, squeaks a couple of times, branches swaying. When she gave a happy hum, he gritted his teeth and looked ruefully down at the bulge that made the pants even tighter.

Damn, he wanted to see her naked. Touch her, kiss her, hear another hum like that when he made love—no, damn it—*pleasured* her.

Love had nothing to do with it.

The rustle of fabrics told him she was getting dressed again. Adam made himself think about their grisly tasks of this morning, and the perilous days ahead.

His body grudgingly accepted his changed mood, but at least he was able to stand up when she returned, to take the saucepan from her and fill it with water on the stove.

EVEN AS SHE pretended to read, all Claire could think about was the dead man when they had pushed him underwater and lowered rocks on top of him. Adam had gently closed Kyle's eyes before they picked him up, but she kept imagining him staring up through the water at her.

It didn't help that the next thing she'd done was inspect Adam's wounds before covering them again and pulling the vet wrap around his chest again. She thought they were healing; neither hole had turned flaming red or seeped pus, but they were still gruesome. Between the gun-shot wound and the cold water, he'd come so close to dying. She kept sneaking peeks at him, picturing him laid out on the beach, marble pale as she'd first seen his face, utterly still, beyond reach.

Adam appeared to be reading, close to finishing *The Mote in God's Eye*. She made a point of turning a page regularly, hoping he hadn't noticed her occasional shudder. If he was really concentrating on the story, he must have better vision than she did. The light was really lousy. It almost felt as if they were in a cave, surrounded on every side by vegetation. What sunlight did reach them had been filtered through the over-reaching spruce and firs that turned it green. If only her electronic reader hadn't reached the end of its charge…

"You've got to think about something else," Adam said gruffly, breaking the lengthy silence. "We made the best decision we could."

She bobbed her head. "I know." And she did, but—"I've never seen anyone dead before."

His surprise was obvious. "Really? Not a grandparent, or—"

"Mike." Wow, the memory of her last glimpse of him made her teeth want to clank together. "I guess I saw him dead."

"He had to have still been aware enough to

release himself from the spray skirt and grab things from that deck pocket after he rolled."

She lifted one shoulder. "Okay, almost dead." Wasn't this a macabre topic. Of course, it had been that kind of day. "Does it…get any easier?"

New tension on his face had her shaking her head. "Forget I asked. You can't possibly want to talk about this."

In the ensuing silence, she didn't look at him.

But then he said haltingly, "I…usually don't."

"I suppose you don't have to with other agents." She hesitated, focusing on a delicate spiderweb strung between two fern fronds. "Assuming you really are a DEA agent. Don't worry—even if you're not, I'll do whatever I can to get us to safety. Then you can just…disappear."

"Claire." He spoke softly, only a little gravel remaining in his voice.

She had to meet his eyes.

"I really am with the DEA. The sooner we can connect with Canadian law enforcement, the better."

That had to be honesty in his eyes. If it wasn't…well, she'd feel really dumb, wouldn't she? But right now, she only nodded.

"As for the dead…" He ran his fingers through his hair. "You're right. We don't talk about it. Mostly, the bodies I've come across were scumbags in real life. Traffickers or muscle sent to intimidate." His shoulders moved. "Users who died from an overdose. Once—" He shook himself. "You don't need to hear about that."

"If you want to talk about it..."

"I don't," he said shortly. "Mostly, in my job you do get inured to it. I've shot and killed four men. Our goal is to arrest them, but things happen."

Like it did on the deck of that freighter, she realized. Undercover, Adam must walk on an edge, knowing his cover could be blown at any minute. Claire couldn't imagine the stress.

"It's not the kind of thing you forget," he continued.

She might be imagining that he was thinking the same she was. That neither of them would forget her friend's death, or Kyle Sheppard's.

When she nodded and stayed silent, he finally went back to his book. Claire went back to pretending.

It wasn't quite dusk when she raised her head. "Listen."

"What?" Adam started to rise to his feet, then stopped. "What the hell?"

"Do you recognize the sound?" She was smiling for the first time since this ordeal had started.

He'd turned toward the beach they could

barely see through the heavy screen of vegetation. "Whales?"

"Yep. Probably orcas. Let's see if they pass in front of us."

She pushed through the branches with him right behind her. From this beach, they had a broader view of the inlet than they'd had at their former campsite. Tinted purple, the sky had deepened the color of the water, too. Looking east, they couldn't see the setting sun.

But she heard again the noisy exhalation made by a whale surfacing for breath, followed by another, and another. As many times as she'd seen orcas, she always got excited. They were magnificent, with their patterns of white against black, the sharp jut of fins and the grace of their massive bodies arching above the water.

Seeing the first one appear, she whispered, "Oh!"

Keeping his voice low, too, as if the creatures would pay the least notice to the humans standing on land, Adam said, "We saw some in the distance on my earlier trip on the freighter. Otherwise, I've never seen an orca."

Soon half a dozen of the pod were visible; others were presumably submerged. They were moving fast, led by the largest, probably a male. By the time she saw the last arching back, the

sky had noticeably darkened. A few more ex-
halations drifted to them, and finally quiet returned with the advent of night.

"They're magnificent," Adam murmured.

She wrinkled her nose. "It's a little unnerving
when one surfaces near your kayak."

"A *little*?"

Still smiling, she said, "Ready for dinner?"

THE BIG MINUS, as far as Adam was concerned,
was that last night, Claire had laid out her own
sleeping bag and pad a foot from his at bedtime,
and without saying a word to him. His sleeping
bag felt cold and unwelcoming with just him in
it. The tree root stretched alongside the edge of
his pad kept him from spreading out. He had a
feeling she hadn't fallen asleep any faster than
he had.

Both of them were quieter than usual over
their morning oatmeal and coffee. She made a
couple of brief suggestions as they packed up.

On the positive side, Adam didn't have to
get wet when he and Claire removed the rocks
weighing down the body and hauled Kyle Sheppard from his temporary watery grave. Adam
tried not to think about the fact that he was wearing the wet suit he'd appropriated. He'd never
robbed the dead before.

And, damn it, he didn't know why he was

giving sentiment any room in his head. It wasn't like him. Practicality was a big component in surviving the dangers of working undercover.

Claire won the argument about who'd climb the cedar tree they chose. It made sense, given that she was less likely to have a limb break under her, and his injury left him debilitated. She went ahead, working her way up as high as she could by stepping from one branch to another and stabilizing herself with a hand on the trunk. Then she tossed an end of a towline they'd tied to a fist-sized rock up and over her chosen limb of the cedar. "Is that high enough?" she called down.

He evaluated the branch. It wasn't twenty feet off the ground, but he didn't see how they could do better. "Yeah. Can you reach the rock?"

"Sure."

She lowered herself carefully, Adam hovering below prepared to catch her, although he hoped she didn't notice. The feathery branches of the cedar shook until she had her feet solidly on the ground.

Adam tied one end of the towline to the dead man's ankles, and then both of them hauled on the other end until the body wedged to a stop. They weren't going to be able to maneuver it over the branch the way Adam had hoped. Making do, he tied the line as securely as possible to a sturdy limb close to the ground. When he stepped back, the body didn't plummet back down.

Good enough.

Claire stared up for a long minute. He saw her throat move, and wondered if she was praying.

They'd already loaded their kayaks and were ready to shove off. Claire hesitated.

"Do you think there's any chance they've given up?"

They hadn't heard the outboard motor yesterday or so far this morning—but yesterday they didn't hear the gunshots, either.

"I want to think so."

She gave a small nod, hearing his doubt, gave her kayak a gentle push and then stepped into the cockpit.

Adam did the same, not looking forward to the day. Claire had insisted on trying something she hoped would help with his shoulder pain, though; using a good-sized book, the BC atlas, and a cutting board, she'd created a stiff cocoon around his shoulder that would accomplish something of the same effect as a plaster cast. Limiting his movement, mostly, forcing him to use his full body to paddle rather than his shoulders. He'd also taken Tylenol, but refused the heavy-duty painkillers in case he needed a clear head.

A moment later, they glided out into a morning he suspected was unusually still. With no breeze, the low-lying fog hadn't broken up into shreds. Claire had a compass mounted to her kayak deck. Without that, Adam couldn't even guess how she'd have navigated. They headed north, their goal a campsite on Spider Island, the largest island in the group.

Even he knew that was a joke. A half-hour outing for a serious kayaker. Another day, he'd asked Claire how far she typically planned to go in a day. Roughly twenty miles, she'd admitted, but she could—and had—exceeded that. The plan for today was two miles, tops. Okay, maybe a little farther than that, given their winding route.

In fact, at the moment, they completed a half circle between smaller islands and the rocky islets that reared from the fog and disappeared as suddenly.

"Stay close," she said one time.

He had no intention of letting her out of his sight. How would he ever find her again? He heard the lap of water against the hull of his kayak, an occasional cry or caw that must be some bird or other overhead. Once a dark head came out of the water so close to him, he could have touched it. An inquisitive face with dark eyes and long whiskers studied him.

A sea otter.

Claire momentarily vanished into the mist, her blue kayak far less visible than his red one. He could see how she'd been able to hide the day her friend was shot. Her neoprene suit was gray and blue, her skullcap navy blue. With her blond hair tucked out of sight, only her yellow flotation vest stood out, and it had either faded or was dirty enough to subdue the bright color.

Adam clung to that thought. She might be able to slip away unseen if he was spotted.

He dug in his paddle to shoot forward and retain his visual on her.

The silence was almost eerie, making him feel as if he wore earmuffs. He started to itch between his shoulder blades, familiar prickles climbing his spine. No reason, he told himself; the fog cloaked them, and they couldn't be tracked by sound. Yet he hated not being able to see more than ten feet in any direction, and kept wondering how much the fog would muffle the noise of a boat motor.

He also began wondering whether the two men he'd seen hunting him—Lee Boyden and Curt Gibbons—were returning to the freighter at night, or making camp somewhere nearby. What if they weren't alone? Another man or two could be taking out the skiff.

How was Dwayne justifying this all-out manhunt to his crew? Adam doubted many, if any of the crew, knew what was at stake.

Adam considered himself damn lucky that the meet had been set up amidst the cluster of islands. The intricate passages were what made this escape possible.

He realized suddenly that Claire must have put on the brakes, because his kayak had glided up beside hers.

"How are you?" she asked.

He had to take a moment to think about it. The pain hadn't immediately hampered him the way it had yesterday.

"Better. Stronger," he decided. He grinned at her. "I think your jury-rigged shoulder harness works."

She laughed. "That's because I'm so smart."

"Has to be," he agreed not quite solemnly.

"I think the fog is starting to lift," she said.

He turned his head. "How can you tell?"

She pointed with her paddle. "See? It's thinner off that way."

"Damn. I like being invisible."

"Well, Spider Island lies off our port side. We'll hug it until we see the inlet where I know there's a campsite."

Adam would have rather aimed for a stop that wasn't listed in maritime guidebooks, but what glimpses he caught of any land seemed to be buttressed by those rock walls rearing from the water. There was nowhere they could pull a kayak ashore.

He cursed his own weakness again.

On that thought, he realized he felt more resistance against his paddle. The tide was still ebbing, but he had no idea what effect that had in a north-south ocean passage between islands. Adam dug in the paddle with more effort and stayed a few feet off the stern of Claire's kayak. She was right—the fog was tearing into long shreds. One moment, the world was gray, the next almost too bright, with glimpses of the blue sky and sun.

They'd been on their way for a couple of hours, at a guess—he'd dropped the wrist watch into the deck hatch to keep it from getting soaked—when he heard a low growling sound.

Swearing, he shot forward again just as Claire's head turned, too.

"That's close," she exclaimed.

"Too damn close. Watch for anyplace we can get out of sight."

She looked scared. "The channel is pretty open here. I don't think we'll be that lucky."

"They may go right by without seeing us."

She gave a sturdy nod and kept paddling, Adam matching her speed even though he was starting to feel as if a spike had been driven through his shoulder.

A shout behind them carried across the water. They'd been seen, and Claire was right—there was no place for them to hide.

Chapter Ten

"Go!" Adam called to Claire. "Don't wait for me!"

Fog again closed around them, all-encompassing gray. He paddled as fast and hard as he could, and hoped she was doing the same. To his frustration, he could still see her. Why wasn't she pulling ahead? Hadn't she taken him seriously?

When they next emerged from the mist, he cast a look over his shoulder. He couldn't see the boat, but the volume of the outboard motor grew. What he'd give for a gun. If they were being pursued by the inflatable, he could capsize it with a few well-placed shots.

His muscles screamed but he didn't ease up. There had to be something he could do to delay these bastards enough for her, at least, to slip away.

Grabbing the flare gun he'd taken from Kyle Sheppard's kayak would require him to quit paddling, if only momentarily. The pocket of his PFD had seemed handy enough, but he'd been wrong.

Using the flare gun—that would mean he had to be within two or three hundred feet, and he had to be able to see the boat. He'd get only one shot, too, so it had to be a good one. If he was in range to use it, they'd sure as hell be in range to shoot him, too, with their far deadlier firearms.

Some distance had opened at last between his kayak and Claire's. She disappeared in fog while he was still in the open, but she yelled something back at him. He couldn't make it out.

He shot into the band of fog and she yelled again. The buzzing from behind grew ever closer, but he heard something else, too. An odd sound. Another boat approaching from the north?

Then she called out again, and this time he heard her. *Orcas.*

That's what he'd heard: the explosive exhalation of an orca. The same pod they'd seen yesterday evening, now turned around to head south?

It came again. A gun fired, too. He was low in the water, which made him a less-than-ideal target. God. What happened if bullets passed through the hull of the kayak? Would he sink? Get dumped back in the bitterly cold water, where he'd wait for death from another bullet…

or death from hypothermia if they didn't see him—or felt especially sadistic?

But he was still moving forward, his level in the water no lower. He rotated his body the way Claire had taught him, going for maximum speed, praying she'd achieved even more.

A bullet skimmed the water to his left even as he heard the report from the gun. Not easy to be accurate when shooting at a moving target from a small craft on the water, he thought, in that remote part of his mind making calculations.

And then water and sound exploded into the air not ten feet to his right, just as a massive black-and-white body leaped out of the water. His rhythm broke. Would one of them come up right *under* him? As close as he and Claire had been on the shore, he hadn't understood how huge these animals were. Would his kayak pass for a seal or whatever these particular orcas hunted?

Or would one come up right under an inflatable boat with a color that would be hard to distinguish from water?

More likely, he thought grimly, the orcas would choose to pass wide around the boat because of the rumble of the motor.

Go, go, go, he ordered himself, not daring to look back. Another back rose a few feet farther away; another spout of water shot into the air.

More, more. A couple of the whales passed to his left. They were splitting to go around him.

The shouts behind him now had a different tone. He hoped Boyden and Gibbons were scared by the killer whales. He hoped this pod was huge.

Instead of pausing to go for the flare gun, he concentrated on paddling for his life. White-hot pain consumed him, but it was a small part of the whole.

Go.

He caught a glimpse ahead of Claire, pausing in her strokes to take a look over her shoulder.

Another orca rose so close by, his kayak rocked and the spout rained on him. He couldn't hear the outboard motor behind him anymore, and finally dared to risk a look back himself. Mist swirled; he saw nothing but whales, beautiful and almost ghostly rising from the water, their spouts joining the mist, the sound of their breaths a powerful symphony.

Adam looked down at the butt of the flare gun, but instead of reaching for it, he resumed paddling.

ADAM'S PROGRESS WAS no longer smooth. Checking frequently behind her, Claire saw that he'd begun a subtle zigzag, inevitably pushed out toward the middle of the passage. Scared, she realized they had to stop, and soon.

The last of the orcas had passed Claire a few minutes ago. She could still hear them, that mysterious, deep blowing that sounded primeval. What she *couldn't* hear was the outboard motor. In their panic, the men might have choked the motor, they might have turned around and fled or the boat might have been overturned by the wave created by a rising or diving orca.

She so wished the last was true, but doubted it would happen. An inflatable boat the size she'd seen would be especially hard to tip.

Even as she paddled for all she was worth, she wished desperately that she'd chosen a different route. This was her fault; the Spider Channel was too open. She'd hoped they would encounter other boaters, but all she'd done was leave Adam and her vulnerable to the men hunting them. Men who could move faster because their boat was motorized.

Maybe they should have gone directly east, except they'd have been even more exposed there, crossing the same anchorage where the freighter and the yacht had met to exchange cargo.

Hurricane Channel would have been good, narrow as it was, with rocks lurking beneath the water at high tide and reputedly choked in with kelp where waters were shallow—except she and Adam would have had to paddle east across Spider Anchorage to reach it.

Same problem.

She strained to hear the motor behind them, but it didn't come. They *had* to get off the water and pray their hunters didn't see the inlet.

There'd been a radar station on Spider Island during World War II, one of a string of them along the Pacific Coast. She'd read that a wooden boardwalk had led from a dock on the west coast of the island to the station, set at a high point. In recent years, the station and boardwalk alike had been overgrown to the point of disappearing. The inlet she was aiming for was now on private land, according to the books she'd read when planning the trip, but right now, she didn't care. They'd be *lucky* if the projected fishing resort had been built. If not—trespassing was the least of their worries.

She kept stealing looks over her shoulder. Adam was falling back, but had her in sight. The water grew rougher as they neared the north end of the island, losing its protection from the open ocean currents and weather patterns. What if they crossed the channel, took a chance that there'd be someplace to pull their kayaks out of the water on Spitfire Island?

Even if their progress was frustratingly slow,

she knew better. Adam needed time to recover. They couldn't go on now.

She saw a cove of sorts and turned toward it. If a fishing resort was under construction, it wasn't here. This was no hidden inlet, either, nor even a beach, but surely they could haul their kayaks and gear over the rocks and hide in the forest.

She waved a paddle. Adam waved back. She still didn't hear any pursuit.

THEY MOVED FAST once they'd managed to beach the kayaks on low-lying slabs of ocean-sculpted rock. Pull out necessary gear, get it above the high-tide line, keep it out of sight in the vegetation. Back for the kayaks, one at a time. Claire slipped on the rocks and would have given in to the injury and exhaustion except they couldn't afford time for whining. She held up her end of Adam's kayak and kept moving.

Once they, the kayaks and their gear were out of sight from the water, Claire collapsed on a rotting log that was probably full of creepy-crawly things, but she was past caring. Adam lowered himself more carefully beside her.

That's when she noticed what looked like the butt of a pistol sticking out of the pocket of his PFD.

Her eyes must have widened.

His gaze followed hers. "Flare gun. Kyle Sheppard's. Remember?"

"Yes. It's just…it looks so much like a gun."

"It *is* a gun. Unfortunately, it shoots a flare instead of a bullet, and has to be reloaded before it can be used again."

"Oh." Of course he was carrying it for its potential as a weapon. "At least it's legal." Heat singed her cheeks. "That's a dumb thing to say. Like that matters." She usually carried one. That, in an effort to lighten her load, she'd figured one flare gun between two people was good enough was just another example of her complacency.

His lips firmed. "If it comes down to us or them, I don't give a damn about the legalities. I feel pretty sure that using it to shoot someone isn't legal."

She'd swear it hadn't been in his pocket when they set out this morning. "That's what you have in mind."

"If need be." His voice and expression both were implacable.

Claire imagined what a flare fired at high speed would do to a human being, but she couldn't work up the horror she should probably feel. Those men had not only shot Adam, they'd been trying to shoot him again today. With bullets. And their guns probably had magazines that allowed for multiple shots before needing to be swapped out.

"What if you shot the boat?" she asked.

"I saw it on the freighter. Didn't look closely, but I doubt it's like the rafts people buy for their kids. You know, the ones that sink after one puncture, or even a little wear and tear. I'm betting an inflatable like this one has compartments. One gets punctured, the boat still floats."

"You're right. I didn't pay that much attention, but I heard a few people talking who had inflatable kayaks. The fabric is really tough, and I think they have multiple valves and separate chambers for air." She frowned. "That means one shot might not even slow them down."

"Right. Although it's possible a flare would penetrate deep enough to do some real damage. Still, I doubt the accuracy is the same as a serious handgun, either." He sounded regretful. "I'd need to be fairly close to take someone out."

"And there are two of them."

He tipped his head but didn't say anything.

"If only I had one, too." *If only* were about the most useless words in the English language.

Eventually, they poked around until they found a relatively flat spot to lay out their sleeping bags or set up a tent, and moved their gear. Adam asked for help removing the makeshift body cast, and after that, they began to unpack what they needed.

Her ankle hurt and she had a bad feeling it was swollen, but she could ignore it, along with the scratches she'd just acquired pushing through branches not eager to give way. There wasn't much she could do about the ankle, for sure, and fortunately, Adam didn't seem to have noticed her favoring that leg. Anyway, if she hurt, he had to be in agony.

They didn't have much view through the dense growth of trees, but they'd hear a motor, and Claire felt sure they'd see anyone dragging a boat up onto the smooth slabs of rock.

Not until she had water on to boil on the small stove did she say, "They have to know more or less where we are."

"Possibly," he said slowly. "That depends what they did when the orcas scared them. They could have tried to get off the water and failed, turned around to run for the ship, or actually suffered enough of a mishap to have a motor that's dead or some other damage to the boat."

She had to say this. "It's my fault we were so out in the open. We can't go back now, but… I've changed my mind about our route."

Furrows deepened in his forehead and between his nose and mouth. He spoke slowly in contrast to what she'd blurted out.

"If we make it out into Queens Sound, you seemed confident there'd be enough traffic, we wouldn't have any trouble waving someone down."

When kayaking up the Inside Passage, she'd gone two or three days at a time without seeing other people, although in those better-traveled waters, she'd had frequent sightings of passing ferries or other large boats in the distance.

She and Mike had chosen to come on this trip early in the season partly because of their jobs, but mostly in hopes of being able to enjoy the beauty of these islands without constant company. By July, there'd be a lot more cabin cruisers, fishing boats and other kayakers. This surprisingly complete solitude...well, she'd have appreciated it in other circumstances.

"Why not go ahead?" Adam asked, after she failed to respond to the last thing he'd said. He'd studied the charts carefully.

Claire took a deep breath. "Because the freighter could be anchored there. As we've been chased north, it would have made sense for your former boss to putter along in the same direction to wait for us. Also, we'd have no place to hide if we're spotted out in the open like that."

"So what are you thinking?"

"Let me grab my charts."

"Water's boiling," he remarked, and they

agreed to eat first. This was early for dinner, but they hadn't had lunch. They could snack closer to bedtime.

She took some ibuprofen, as did he—his a double dose.

When she was able to show him what she had in mind, he leaned forward and traced a fingertip along the narrow, twisting channel that headed east and then sharply south, cutting between several of the larger islands in the area.

"That'll let us out not far from where we started," he said slowly. "What's the point of that?"

"I think it would be unexpected. They've followed us this far. Would they expect us to circle around?"

"You think they can't follow us?"

"I imagine they can, but from what I remember reading, the Spitfire Channel is tricky. It's really narrow at one point, has dangerous submerged rocks, kelp beds that could tangle around the propeller." She hesitated. "There are two problems with going that way."

"Besides going in a circle?"

Claire ignored his comment. "One is that I have no idea whether there are any places at all where we could beach the kayaks until we come out on the other side, and I think that's too far for you to paddle in one day. There almost has to be a possible campsite somewhere, but we'll need to keep a sharp eye or miss our chance."

"And the other problem?"

"Crossing the open water unseen to get to the channel."

He gazed down at the chart for a minute. "What about crossing the channel, then heading north along the shore of this Hunter Island?"

"That's the logical route. They'll think we're running for Bella Bella."

"I take it that's the closest thing to civilization on this part of the coast?"

"Yes, which makes that direction too obvious. We need to do something they won't expect. Just...disappear."

He frowned over the chart for a minute, then nodded. "They didn't spot us for a couple of hours this morning. They may not be early starters."

"No, but I'm more worried because they have to guess we've gone to ground somewhere in this vicinity."

"Then we launch at first light," he said grimly. "Or even earlier."

He was right; they could cross the open channel in the murky, purple light before the sun actually topped the horizon, given the lack of other boat traffic. That meant setting out between four thirty and five o'clock.

"You expect to see more boat traffic in this Kildidt Sound?" he asked.

Claire nodded. "Once we aren't dodging between tiny islands." When he didn't comment, she set aside the charts and put more water on to heat to wash their dishes.

Watching out of the corner of her eye as Adam brooded, she decided not to mention another issue: Hunter and Hurricane Islands must boast plentiful wildlife, including the bears and wolves smart campers avoided.

IN THE LATE AFTERNOON, a cloud of insects found them.

They'd been incredibly lucky so far not to have to crouch under netting to keep from being eaten alive.

"Son of a bitch," Adam growled, hearing the first whine. "I hate mosquitoes."

"They're not alone. I think those are midges, too. Their bites are even more irritating."

Claire dug hurriedly in a bag and came up with some netting and a baseball cap. "You take this. Wrap the netting around your head."

Adam clapped the baseball cap on his head. "What about you?"

"I have another one." She found it, and a pair of thin gloves. "Look through your bag. Mike carried these, too. They're actually glove liners."

Momentarily protected with no skin exposed, he still swatted irritably at the cloud of bugs swarming them. He swore he itched even if he hadn't been bitten. "Don't you have some repellent?"

"No, it can melt synthetic material. Plus, the smell attracts bears."

"Great."

"We'll have to set up the tent. It has netting."

He hadn't noticed, but was glad to hear it.

"We might as well do that now." She stood suddenly. "I'll be back in a minute."

She'd already pushed her way through the evergreen branches and lower-growing bushes that blocked them from the beach before he could get to his feet. Surprised and uneasy, Adam followed her.

Head tipped back, she was looking at the sky. When he did the same, he saw that it was no longer clear the way it had been. The air felt different, too, he realized. Damp.

"Can we take off in the morning if it's raining?"

"It'll depend."

About to ask on what, he stiffened. "Hear that?"

"Oh, no," she whispered.

"You have the binoculars handy?"

She ducked back the way she'd come and

handed them to him. They both crouched behind a veil of low cedar limbs and waited.

That damn inflatable boat appeared, moving slowly along the shoreline. Adam lifted his netting to use the binoculars. It had come almost abreast of them when he realized he'd left the flare gun at the campsite.

Don't look this way.

Damn, he wished for twilight.

The boat kept going until it was out of sight. Not sure he'd taken a breath, Adam pulled in a deep one and yanked the netting down.

Neither he nor Claire moved, both listening to the receding sound of the motor. They heard it for a while, continuing north, until it either faded away or was cut off.

He swore. "Is there another campsite up there?"

"I think there must be." She was almost whispering. "I was aiming for one that has to be better than landing on rocks. You think…?"

"You know as much as I do," he said shortly, immediately regretting his tone when she stood up and pushed her way back toward their camp.

By the time he got there, she was packing away the pan, stove and dishes for the night, so practiced at it he didn't bother to offer to help.

Damn. He hated feeling completely inept. He'd been stuck in some tight places before, but he'd never been so outside his areas of expertise. Yeah, he was getting better with the kayak, but he didn't kid himself for a minute that he could handle anything but the placid seas they'd so far traversed, and that in slo-mo. If his kayak rolled, he'd hang there head down until he drowned.

He knew nothing about navigating or about the dangers in this wild part of the world. Babe in the woods, that was him.

Which left him utterly dependent on the gutsy woman who'd saved his life and was serving as his guide, trusting him even though she had no reason to believe a word he'd said.

The woman he would do anything at all to protect from the consequences of her courageous act. He'd like to think that was out of gratitude and because it was part of his job as a federal law enforcement officer, but knew better.

This woman had gotten to him in a short time, as he'd never allowed anyone to do. These feelings baffled and alarmed him, but he had to acknowledge them. The sooner he got away from her, the better…but he'd like to hold her in his arms every one of the remaining nights before he had to let her go back to her formerly safe life.

His mouth twisted. Too bad he knew what she'd say if he suggested sharing a sleeping bag again.

Smart woman.

Chapter Eleven

They went to work raising the tent. As irritating as the swarming insects were, Adam was about ready to crawl into it, however cramped the quarters, zip the flap closed and huddle there until morning.

This task was another one he had to leave mostly to Claire, exacerbating his mood. As little as he'd paddled, he was developing some blisters. Probably gripping the paddle too tightly, a mistake that could have several unpleasant consequences. They had yet to camp anywhere Claire could drive stakes; instead, the tent had to be secured by lines tied to nearby tree limbs. Given the lack of mobility in his right arm and the blisters, he was lousy at dealing with the thin cord.

Yeah, he could have done it, but would have taken twice as long. One more source of frustration.

Given their relative sizes, he gave up and let

her crawl inside and lay out the pads and sleeping bags, too. She didn't suggest they head right to bed, though, only crawled back out.

Apparently, she wasn't any readier to drop into peaceful slumber than he was, and didn't favor squatting in the tent until she was.

Net masking his face, Adam sat down on that too-low-to-the-ground chair and resumed brooding.

"What are you thinking?" Claire asked at last.

"Wishing we could have holed up at either of our previous campsites," he said honestly. "Someone would have come along eventually. And yeah, I know that wasn't possible."

They'd come too close once to being discovered at the first campsite. If the boat had circled closer, one of the men would have seen the break in the rock guarding the island. No matter what, the diminishing supply of drinking water would have forced them to move on.

He slapped a mosquito that had settled on a strip of skin between his cuff and glove.

Lingering at the inlet where they found Sheppard's body would have been too risky, too. It would have been logical for Adam's former shipmates to revisit it. Adam wasn't crazy about tonight's, either, even if they were hidden in the woods. What they weren't was in a good position to put a kayak in the water fast to intercept a passing boat they could be sure had no connection to the freighter or the yacht.

What ate at him was how many days had gone by. Had the yacht slunk back to finish taking on the remaining cargo? Or was he wrong, and it had already loaded the important and dangerous part?

"Damn, I wish we knew if they'd set up camp," he said aloud. "The flare gun isn't much use, but I could slash that damn boat with a knife and make sure they couldn't ever launch it again."

She turned her head to stare at him, alarm in her eyes. "Just tiptoe up and start poking holes?"

"Something like that."

"You don't think the air rushing out wouldn't make noise? Sort of like the orcas exhaling?"

He unclenched his teeth. "It might. Wouldn't take me long, though."

"I wish I thought you were just dreaming."

"I have trouble believing they're going back to the freighter every night. The smaller boat coming and going might draw unwelcome attention. A rusty old tub like that is in danger of catching the eye of the coast guard as it is. If they see it twice…why is it just sitting there?"

"Good reason for them to be moving around, except they almost have to be staying out in deeper waters most of the time." She sounded thoughtful. "They might have anchored in Fulton Passage, but if they're really following us north, they'd have had to follow the western shore of Spider Island."

"The two guys we've seen—" he told her their names, not sure he had before "—must have radio contact with the freighter, but they might be afraid to go back in person and admit to Dwayne that they can't seem to find us. Or, now, that they did, but let us get away."

"Because a bunch of orcas got in the way."

Adam grinned, knowing the expression wasn't a nice one. "Dwayne wouldn't have much patience if they make up stories like that."

"It was sort of surreal."

"Yeah. That's the word I was trying to think of. Between the fog and the gunshots following us, their appearance seemed…" He hesitated.

Claire supplied a word. "Magical."

Adam couldn't argue with her, although that wasn't a word that had ever crossed his lips.

"Well, right now, you have no idea where those guys are camped for the night," she said briskly. "So you can put out of your mind any fantasies of slashing their boat to ribbons. I'm not volunteering to head back out on the water to look for them."

"I wouldn't take you if you did."

He didn't have to see her to know she was glaring at him. His very silence let her know she'd won this argument. No, he wasn't stupid enough to set out as dark gathered hoping to see the light of a campfire or kerosene lantern.

That didn't mean he put the idea out of his head.

CLAIRE CRAWLED INTO her sleeping bag, lay still for about ten seconds, then squirmed in search of a more comfortable position. The loamy soil had seemed to pad the spot where she'd positioned the tent, but she should have realized how many tree roots reached and tangled beneath the surface. She might as well be stretched out on crisscrossing iron bars. This was like an ancient sleeper sofa with about a two-inch thick mattress, except she couldn't seem to find anywhere to settle her butt and shoulder simultaneously *between* roots.

"You okay?" Adam's gritty voice came out of the darkness.

"Sure. Just... There's a tree root right under me." Or two or three—or ten. She shifted to her left, then tried to scrunch herself up against the back wall of the tent.

"Scoot over closer to me," he suggested.

She wanted to, so much she knew it wasn't a good idea. But she wouldn't be sleeping at all if she didn't get more comfortable. So she rolled once, sleeping bag and all, until she came up against a hard body. Claire held still for a long moment.

"Better?"

"I think so. I'm afraid to move."

His low chuckle might be the sexiest sound she'd ever heard.

"Here." After some rustling, a long arm wrapped around her and pulled her even closer. She could rest her head on his shoulder, and would have been able to lay an arm across his chest and a leg over his, if the bulk of two sleeping bags hadn't separated them. She suddenly regretted that barrier.

"Warm enough?" His breath tickled her hair.

"Uh-huh." Too warm, which was his fault.

"Sleep tight, sweetheart."

She froze, and thought he'd gone completely still, too. She'd swear he had quit breathing. Had that just slipped out?

If so, he'd surprised himself, and not in a good way.

But he didn't say anything, and she didn't move. Eventually she did drop off to sleep, although she felt like it wasn't that long before she woke up again. Apparently she'd moved enough to find a new lump. She had to squirm some, waking him, although all he did was mumble, "Wha's wrong?"

"Nothing. Just…" Turning over? No, she couldn't do that. She wriggled a little, fell back asleep. Woke up again, tried rolling away from Adam, but had to go back where she'd started from.

The next time she woke up, it was because she heard rustling accompanied by heavy breathing outside the tent. Even in the dark, she saw the side push in as something leaned against it.

Claire became aware that Adam's entire body was rigid. "What the…?" he murmured.

"Bear," she whispered in his ear. "I think."

Snuffling noises and a grunt confirmed her fear. She grabbed the can of bear spray, but once she had it in hand, she continued to lie still, glad Adam did the same.

Neither of them had spilled any food, had they? Was the smell of their dinner lingering in the air? It had been vegetarian, thank goodness, nothing that should have attracted any particular attention. They'd set the food vaults a fair distance away.

Another grunt, more rustling…and silence. Claire listened for all she was worth, but couldn't hear anything except…

"Is that rain?" Adam asked quietly.

"I think so." It was a little hard to tell for sure, because they were protected by such dense forest. Instead of pattering onto the tent—or hammering—they were getting the drips filtered through multiple layers of tree branches. "Oh, joy."

"Good thing we set up the tent," Adam commented. "For more than one reason."

He was right; she definitely wouldn't have wanted to wake up to a curious bear snuffling in her face.

Even thinking about water falling from the sky caused her bladder to suggest that she make a trip outside, but she'd have had to be a lot more desperate to obey. As Adam said, for more than one reason.

Somehow, she fell asleep again, and he must have, too, because she was half lying on top of him when she opened her eyes again to gray light and a strong neck and throat.

Dark stubble was becoming a beard. Would it be wiry or soft? She was suddenly breathing a little faster. If she lifted her head from his shoulder the tiniest bit, she could press her lips to his neck…

She'd either shocked herself, or come completely awake, because her next, more coherent thought was, so much for that early departure.

And now she *really* needed to put some clothes on and get out of the tent so she could pee.

He protested when she rolled off him and started squirming into the garments she'd kept in the sleeping bag with her so they wouldn't be miserably cold this morning.

"Gotta get up," she told him, pulling a fleece top over her shirt.

He groaned. "I wish you hadn't said that."

As she scooted out of the tent, she heard him scrambling into clothes behind her.

Ugh. Straightening in the clearing, she felt as if she were breathing water. Yes, it was still raining, and every branch and fern frond dripped. She heard movement up above, too: the wind that had been absent for most of the past week.

Claire pushed her way through the soggy vegetation to find a spot to crouch, then made her way back. No Adam, so she stepped out of the trees to find choppy waves not far from her feet. This had *not* been an ideal place to stop and set up camp.

Looking out at the channel, she knew there was no way they could set out today. On her own, she'd have hesitated. For an inexperienced kayaker, it was impossible.

Her first awareness that Adam had joined her was his growled profanity, followed by, "We're stuck."

"We've been lucky with the weather so far," she pointed out.

"What if this lasts for days?"

Droplets clung to his dark hair and dampened

his face. Muscles flexed in his jaw as he stared out at the choppy waters.

"What do you think? We sit here. We have enough food and drinking water, and could catch some rain if need be."

Boredom and this unwanted sexual attraction would be the biggest threats, she thought.

Still glowering at the channel, he said, "Damn!"

"We have a couple of tarps we can tie over the campsite so at least we don't get any wetter than we already are," she offered.

He growled, "That'll be cozy."

Finally getting mad, Claire punched his upper arm and snapped, "Suck it up."

ADAM FOLLOWED HER to the kayaks and delved into the hatches on his own kayak while she did the same on hers. He should be grateful that he still had plenty of dry garments, he told himself. A day resting up wouldn't be the end of the world.

Immediately, he wished he'd chosen a better way to phrase the thought. No, the uranium being smuggled wasn't enough to end the world, but it could blast a significant part of it. A military base? A city? He'd give a lot to know the target of the terrorists who could, even now, be assembling their bomb.

He had to remind himself that, even if he

knew more, there wasn't a damn thing he could do about it. What they'd needed was some early intelligence so they could have prevented the freighter ever leaving the harbor.

All he could do now was dial down his disagreeable mood, however justified it was, and accept that he was no superhero. Nature had given him a slap to remind him of her supremacy.

He wondered how stormy the seas were out in the open ocean. The picture of the freighter rising and sliding down twenty-foot-high swells gave him some pleasure. Everyone on board violently seasick. Anything on deck washed overboard.

Except maybe for the uranium. He wasn't sure what would happen with it sitting on the ocean floor. It might be an environmental disaster.

He and Claire hung the three big tarps they'd located over the tent and the rest of the campsite, using cords and even a towline through grommets to tie the corners to branches.

Neither of them said much while she cooked up a pan of their usual oatmeal, adding dried cranberries to it this morning instead of the usual raisins or nuts. Only when she handed him a mug of coffee did he say, "I'm sorry for the whining."

She raised her eyebrows. "Is that what it was?"

Then she relented. "I understand your sense of urgency."

"You know any prayers for good weather? Or what about a dance?"

Her chuckle brightened her face and his mood both. "Nothing I've ever tried has worked. Sorry." She chewed on her lower lip for a minute, watching him without quite meeting his eyes. "You know, I've gotten caught out on more turbulent water than this and lived to tell about it. I could make a run for it while you—"

"Not a chance," he interrupted. Coffee splashed onto his hand as he glowered at her. "Do you seriously think I'll let you lay your life on the line while I hunker down here...doing what? Catching up on my reading?"

"But every day counts," she said quietly.

She was right. He remembered thinking that he could end up having to sacrifice her to save the hundreds to thousands of people that damn bomb would kill. Collateral damage, a concept he'd had to consider before while working undercover. What might have been thinkable on day one had become a hell, no.

"It would take you longer to get results," he said, still looming over her. "If I'm there, things will move faster."

"A whole day faster?"

No, but he felt sick at the idea of seeing her

paddling away, the frail kayak tossing on waves capable of flipping it. Her disappearing in the rain; him not knowing whether she'd made it. Given the weather, what were the odds she'd meet up with other boaters? Even large cabin cruisers or fishing boats would surely stay anchored in sheltered inlets. Struggling on her own, how long would it take her to pop out in Kildidt Sound, somehow signal as big a boat as possible to stop in the gray, slanting rain and wait for a representative of the Canadian Coast Guard or Navy?

Or *she* could go north and strike boldly out into Queens Sound. Where, lacking any electronic devices, she'd have only flares for signaling for help. If the pilot of a large ship miscalculated the origin of the flare, that ship could just as well run right over the top of her—especially if the ocean and sky were both still gray, swells sometimes hiding her kayak.

No.

CLAIRE WASN'T ABOUT to tell him how grateful she was that he'd nixed her suggestion. So, okay, she was scared, but she still thought splitting up might be the smart thing to do. Even if the two men from the freighter came upon her, why would they do anything but exchange the time of day with her and ask if she'd seen a guy in a red kayak?

Unless they saw her yesterday paddling hard not that far ahead of Adam.

Yes, but would they go out in such miserable weather? A lot of people, even sailors, got seasick when such a small boat was tossed around.

Adam obviously considered the argument over. He dug in one of the dry bags and produced the short stack of books. He didn't seem excited by any of them, but finally started reading. Claire followed suit, although it was hard to concentrate on her last unread book, a British procedural mystery. So what if she wasn't in the mood for it?

Thanks to the addition of poor Kyle Sheppard's stash, they had meals aplenty, enough that she heated a vegetarian chili for lunch instead of the cold alternatives.

Adam accepted a bowl from her and inhaled the spicy scent. "This isn't an invitation to last night's visitor?"

"No meat. I doubt chili pepper and cumin smell appealing to a black bear."

"That was a bear."

"Yes. There might be wolves on the island, but they don't snuffle and grunt."

"Think it'll be back?"

She waggled a hand. "I imagine it stumbled on us, but it didn't find anything appealing."

He grimaced.

For some reason, Claire smiled at his expression. "I take it you're not into nature?"

"No. City all the way."

The mood changed as he haltingly told her more about his background. Claire learned that he'd grown up in Dallas, which admittedly felt like a world away from this wild, rainy edge of North America. His voice sounded rusty as he talked about his childhood and eventually how he'd ended up in law enforcement. He gazed more at the stove, as if it was a crackling blaze, than he did at her.

He admitted to half a dozen foster homes. With the last, he got lucky. The foster father was a Texas marshal.

"Not…fatherly, but he pushed me toward college. Helped me find scholarships. I don't know if he saw something in me. I wanted to think so. I tried some classes in criminology. Took enough for a minor." He flicked a glance at her. "Majored in chemistry."

He'd mentioned starting as a chemist.

"Did you stay in touch with your foster dad?" she asked gently.

"First year." There was a long pause. "Then he started sounding impatient. He and his wife were fostering a brother and sister they'd taken in after I was out of the house." He shrugged. "I took the hint."

"Are you sure that's what it was?"

Seeing the look on his face, she was immediately sorry she'd pushed.

"He never called again."

Struck by the way he'd said, *his wife*, Claire wondered what kind of relationship Adam had with her. Not much of one, if she had to guess.

"So you went to the DEA."

"Yeah. It seemed like a good fit."

Chemistry and criminology. Of course it was.

"You've never been married?"

Deepened furrows on his forehead made her wonder what he was thinking. But then he said, "With my history, I've…had a hard time imagining it. Never met the right woman, anyway, which was probably just as well considering what I do for a living."

She couldn't be surprised by his attitude. Saddened, maybe. She couldn't tell him that in so few days, he was responsible for her being able to dismiss even the smallest regret about Devin.

Adam's profession didn't overshadow all the qualities she'd seen in him: determination, reliability, kindness, patience, a sense of humor. Would he ever recognize how much he had to offer a woman?

Probably not.

A secret part of her remembered how desperate he'd been yesterday for *her* to escape, even if those creeps caught up to him.

Because she could carry his message to the proper authorities?

Yes, but he'd seemed curious about her, too, and hadn't been anything but kind and thoughtful. Even...tender, although that had to be her imagination.

Wow, there were a lot more important things for her to be thinking about than this ridiculous attraction to him. Even if they were spending the day in close proximity, and she'd have no choice but to sleep pressed up against him.

She went back to listening for any sounds that didn't belong and pretending she didn't notice the thoughtful way he was now watching her. Finally, Claire picked up her book and did her absolute best to be gripped by adventures that paled by comparison with everything that had happened to *her* in the past few days.

Chapter Twelve

If they'd been exploring the islands for fun, the day might have been relaxing. Say, if this were Claire and her buddy. They'd obviously been good enough friends, with enough history, to enjoy hanging out and talking. Under the circumstances, would she have slept cuddled up to her partner Mike instead of to Adam?

Adam was immediately ashamed of himself, considering that her friend was dead, his body adrift. Murdered because he'd inadvertently stepped into the middle of Adam's investigation.

He frowned. That wasn't quite true. If the DEA had never succeeded in inserting an agent on that boat, Dwayne would have shot the poor guy anyway.

Unless he was on edge more than usual because he'd begun to suspect I wasn't what I appeared.

Adam told himself to knock it off. The nature of his job was that anything could happen, and he couldn't take responsibility for all of it. He mixed with suspicious, volatile, violent people who lacked any semblance of empathy.

Unfortunately, his thoughts circled back to how much he wanted Claire. *You can't have her. Live with it.*

Several times during the night, he'd surfaced to find himself holding her, her breath tickling his neck, and he'd been thrown back to remembering the nights when they'd shared a sleeping bag and he'd been aware of all her curves pressed against him. When he could so easily have—

He slammed that door shut. No, he couldn't have, not given what bad shape he was in then, not given his awareness that this woman had saved his life at great peril to herself. Even more important, she was grieving for her friend, and had to be a lot more scared than she let him see.

This was not the time and place for what he'd been thinking.

The way she looked at him sometimes, though…

He shook his head, then hoped she hadn't noticed. If he could just go for a long walk. Have a hard workout. Anything to take his mind off her, give his restlessness an outlet. Instead, they were trapped in a space that wasn't more than ten square feet that encompassed bedroom, kitchen and sitting room. They were almost always close enough to each other to touch, if they chose.

If she asked him what he was thinking right now, he didn't know what he'd do. Kiss her, he was afraid, and not gently.

They read again that afternoon. If anything, the rain had picked up, although the tide did recede so their home-away-from-home wasn't quite so alarmingly waterfront.

Bored with his book, he asked if she carried any games.

"I'm afraid not," she said regretfully. "That might have been smart. My other trips with Mike were shorter, and usually it was all we could do to set up camp, have a meal and get to bed early enough to set out at the crack of dawn the next day. If Mike had cell phone coverage, he'd call his wife. The two of us are—" she choked on that "—we *were* both big readers, so…" Claire let that trail off.

"Just a thought. You know his wife pretty well?"

"Yes. I met Mike in a kayaking class, and once he introduced me to Shelby, we hit it off. We're…really good friends. I'm so dreading—" She didn't want to finish that sentence, either.

"She must know by now that something is wrong," he said quietly.

Claire's mouth twisted. "Maybe. His SPOT is

being pulled around by the tide and currents, you know. Either…with his body, or not. The signal might be moving weirdly, or showing up out in the ocean farther from land than we should be, but she knows we intended to take our time and wander. She could still be telling herself that he's out of cell phone range. That happens."

"We *are* out of cell phone range." Adam had seen her check her phone twice today. He hadn't had to tell her that the weather probably wasn't helping.

"What's Shelby like?" he asked, not sure why he wanted to know. Except he did know; if Claire had been his wife, he wouldn't have been okay with her heading off for a couple of weeks' trip to the back of beyond with another man.

"She's wonderful." Claire visibly relaxed. "Dramatic, funny, smart. Gorgeous, too. The first time I met her, I felt squat and plain in comparison, but Shelby isn't constantly aware of herself the way I might expect someone with her beauty to be. She's a redhead with masses of wild, curly hair and an hourglass figure. And not a single freckle."

His eyebrows rose. "Because she stays out of the sun?"

"Probably. She's not the outdoorsy type, that's for sure. Well, that isn't true. Last winter, she and Mike went to Barbados for two weeks and sounded like they had a fabulous time. Some-how, she came home without more than a hint of a tan and still with *no freckles*."

Adam laughed. "Don't like your own freck-les much?"

She crinkled her nose. "I'm resigned. You can probably tell I don't tan at all—I just burn no matter how much suntan lotion I plaster on. Which also doesn't keep me from getting freck-les."

He grinned at her. "I can barely see them through the sunburn. When you peel, do the freckles go, too?"

"Nope." She laughed at herself. "I don't actu-ally care if I have them or not. I don't love slath-ering myself with suntan lotion and then aloe vera, so I'm greasy all the time, and still know-ing I'll go through that awful peeling and itch-ing phase. Plus..." She hesitated.

"You need to start thinking about skin can-cer."

He hadn't meant to sound so stern, earning a startled look from her.

After a minute, she said, "I don't know if sea kayaking will ever give me the same joy again. Although, I do love being in the middle of na-ture instead of concrete. You know?"

He'd never thought about it before, but this experience seemed to be altering his perspective. If he and Claire were lovers, paddling between the islands for fun, marveling at sights like the pod of orcas, sharing life stories and the small touches that would lead well into nighttime passion... Yeah, he thought he could be happy.

He couldn't offhand remember the last time he had been.

"You'll remember the good times," he said, as if he were spouting the pat lines from a greeting card, "and let go of the grief."

She snorted. "You mean, seeing what a bullet does to a man's head? I don't think so."

"I'm sorry you got caught up in this."

The filtered green light here under the trees altered the vivid blue of her eyes. The eyes that held his. "That, I don't regret. If I hadn't been here, *you'd* be dead, too."

Staggered, he didn't move. She almost sounded as if his death would have hit her as hard as her friend's. Harder.

She wouldn't have known me, he reminded himself.

Adam had a little trouble remembering how he'd felt before *he* met *her.*

On a scrabble of panic, he picked up his book again, opened it and stared sightlessly at the page.

So much for relaxation.

As far as Claire was concerned, the day had been interminable. She was grateful for the distraction of preparing dinner and cleaning up afterward. She and Adam returned to the rocky shore, only to find an angry tide devouring the rocks, but the rainfall seeming lighter.

"Maybe there's hope," Adam growled, and left her standing there.

His mood had been up and down all day; he'd go from friendly to withdrawn within seconds. It had to be intense frustration and impatience, nothing to do with her, but she didn't like it. She wished she thought she could sneak away in the morning, but knew better.

She also seriously considered finding a softer piece of ground where she could spread out her mat and sleeping bag, rain or no rain, but remembering the visitor last night cured her of that foolishness. A curious bear was liable to wander by again to see what these strange creatures were up to. And then there were the bugs.

With a sigh, she turned to follow Adam.

He had the wristwatch in his hands. She didn't want to ask, but couldn't help herself.

"What time is it?"

"Eight. If we're going to get up at—what?— four in the morning, we should probably hit the sack."

She'd almost gotten used to going to bed in bright daylight. The tent was a big help, dimming the light enough to fool her circadian rhythms. Most nights on a trip like this, she was exhausted by a long day on the water and the work of setting up camp. She hadn't just *sat* all day.

"I'll keep the watch close along with the flashlight," Adam said. "I wish I could set an alarm, but I'm usually pretty good at setting an internal one. Last night...wasn't like me. If there's any chance it quits raining, we can get that early start."

"Fine." If that sounded snippy, so be it.

She set about heating water, and carried the pan and a washcloth, soap and towel behind the tent, where she could take what Mike had called a sponge bath. A hasty one, given the insect life. When she came back, Adam said, "Good idea."

He took the saucepan from her hand, filled it with water and pulled out his own bathing supplies.

He wasn't really out of sight behind the tent, but he didn't strip down any more than she had. While he scrubbed his underarms, Claire brushed her teeth and hung the dry bag with her toiletries from a high branch. Not that she thought bears would like the smell of soap—a bar that was citrus scented—or toothpaste, but they could be nosy and she didn't want her possessions scattered. Or a claw through her toothpaste tube.

Maybe if she hustled, she could move her sleeping bag onto his mat and vice versa, and be sound asleep before he decided to go to bed.

Or pretend to be.

But she had no doubt he'd be right on her heels, so instead she stayed on her hands and knees and tried to find a corner in the tent where she might be able to wedge herself to sleep.

"You know," he said right behind her, "if we shared a sleeping bag again, we could put both mats and the extra sleeping bag beneath us. We might actually be comfortable."

"No."

"Was it that bad?"

Of course not. But that was then, this was now.

"The stress is getting to me." His voice was a note lower, a quiet rumble. "I know I've snapped at you a few times today."

Claire swiveled and plopped her butt down so she could see him. Adam was crouched just inside the tent opening, his elbows braced on his thighs. The position stretched the fabric of his cargo pants taut over long muscles and made her very aware of his hands dangling between his thighs.

"I don't mind the snapping," she said honestly. "I don't like doors slammed in my face."

He didn't so much as blink for a minute. "I... didn't realize I was doing that."

"It's not like I can take my toys and go home."

Furrows deepened on his forehead. "I'd hate it if you did that. I'm...grateful for your company even if I wish all this hadn't put you at risk, too."

She sighed. "We shouldn't share a sleeping bag."

He let his head drop forward. "I want you."

Electrified by a zing of shock, she stared at him. He'd come right out and said what she'd guessed even as she doubted herself. "This... isn't good timing," she said, barely above a whisper.

When he lifted his head, his eyes burned into hers. "I know that. Believe me. I wouldn't push you. I won't." One side of his mouth tipped up in an almost smile. "Whichever one of us was on the bottom would probably end up with a few broken vertebrae anyway."

She frowned at him to cover the continuing shock and startling arousal. "I thought your mat was laid out on flat ground."

A flash of humor made her heart clench.

"Are you kidding? I'm just used to...shutting out discomfort." He shrugged.

Claire laughed despite everything. "Gee, your suggestion that I sleep with you is even more irresistible."

"You could sleep on top of me," he said roughly.

She almost whimpered. "I sort of did last night," she admitted.

"I know."

That gritty admission sent her into a meltdown she absolutely could not afford. She didn't really *know* this man. Even if he was all he professed to be, that meant he was a loner, damaged by a childhood lacking in love and security, a guy with a dangerous job that would have him gone for weeks or months at a time, and that was assuming he worked out of Seattle and not... She didn't know. Anchorage? San Francisco? Miami?

And, okay, she had some vanity issues. Despite what she could do with a washcloth, she needed a hot shower or bath to shave her legs and underarms. Not how she'd want him to see—or feel—her the first time.

"I think I'd better stay in my own sleeping bag," she said, her voice huskier than usual.

The heat in his eyes didn't diminish, but after a moment he nodded. "I'll give you a few minutes of privacy."

"Thanks."

He backed out, leaving her alone.

ADAM DETERMINED TO keep the bear spray close that night. Turned out, he didn't have to look for either; Claire had placed both in easy reach for either of them.

And no, she couldn't be asleep, but she stayed absolutely still as he slipped into his sleeping bag beside her. He lay there wondering if the spray was any more useful than pepper spray that was known to just enrage a human assailant. Not that he and Claire had any other weapons or deterrents to chase a bear away. From what he'd read, not even a handgun was an answer. Grizzlies, at least, were hard to bring down. Bullets from a pistol might be the equivalent of a few bee stings.

He forced himself to think about tomorrow. His shoulder had ached less than he'd expected from yesterday's exertions. Of course, they hadn't been on the water long at all, but he'd sure as hell tried to hurry, forgetting any of the technique that Claire had tried to drum into him.

He told himself he shouldn't have any trouble paddling across the channel to the island on the other side and finding a campsite. He'd like to think it would be that easy, but Boyden and Gibbons had popped up every time he and Claire made a move. If they'd camped versus returning to the freighter, they couldn't be that far away. Adam would give a lot to know where they were.

He and Claire at least had the advantage that the kayaks were silent and low enough in the water to make spotting them more difficult. Too bad they couldn't summon the pod of orcas again.

It took a while, but he finally thought he could sleep. He hoped so; he'd been trying not to move around despite the ridges digging into his back, butt and even calves. Claire remained so damn still, he knew she wasn't asleep, either. Adam had hoped she would drop off so he could relax, but maybe it had to work in reverse. His wounded body probably required more sleep than usual to heal, too.

When his eyes snapped open, full night had fallen. He'd heard something…

It almost sounded like a voice, deep throated and demanding. Hell. He started to sit up, reaching automatically for the weapon that should be under his pillow, but Claire's hand gripped his arm.

"Bear," she whispered.

The sounds continued. Then she said something a lot more alarming. "Bears."

Plural.

Scrabbling sounds followed. Claws digging into bark?

Adam seized the spray bottle. It was like facing off with a guy carrying a semiautomatic when all you had was a starter's pistol. Feeling completely vulnerable did not sit well with him.

Scuffling, the shaking of vegetation, and something crashed into the side of the tent, pushing it inward. Low, not high like a full-grown bear's rump bumping the fabric wall. It wasn't trying to dig them out, was it?

More vocalization. He heard sounds coming from in front of the tent and off to the side.

Claire leaned so close her lips tickled his ear. Her voice was almost soundless. "I think that's a mom and cubs."

Cubs that might have been wrestling and rolled against the tent wall. Hell. Mom had to know he and Claire were right here. Didn't bears have poor vision and rely instead on a powerful sense of smell?

Claire still leaned on him, her fingertips biting into his forearm. Okay by him. His heart slammed against his rib cage. This form of danger was way out of Adam's frame of reference. Maybe they should start shouting and make a racket to try to scare the bears away, but he trusted Claire's knowledge of local wildlife. The decision was hers.

More snuffles, grunts and something that was almost a squeak. Mother bear giving orders that were being protested?

He and Claire remained absolutely still. If she

was breathing, he couldn't hear it. Adam had done plenty of stakeouts, but he didn't remember ever staying so rigid for such a length of time.

A branch cracked under pressure. Others swished back and forth. Eventually, there was silence. Even then he didn't move, straining for the slightest sound.

"Oh, my God." Claire let go of him and collapsed back onto her mat.

Adam groaned. He had no idea how much time had passed since he'd opened his eyes, but he was betting it had been fifteen minutes or more.

"That was scary," Claire suggested.

He looked down at her, tracking her voice, because he sure couldn't see her.

"Damn right."

Suddenly, she was giggling.

He couldn't help himself. He bent over her, succeeded despite the darkness in finding her mouth. He had to kiss her. His tension had built for days, and now that band had snapped. Rebounded.

He wasn't as gentle as he should have been. When her lips parted, he dove in, his tongue plunging into the soft depths of her mouth. His hands clamped to each side of her head before one slid beneath her neck to squeeze the muscles. Incoherent sounds broke from her, and she'd grabbed hold of him, too, a hand squeezing his upper arm, the other finding the muscle that ran from his neck to his shoulder.

He'd have given damn near anything to be able to *see* her, but they grappled in complete darkness. He rolled to his shoulder and took her with him. She said his name before stinging his lip with her teeth. When he shoved down her sleeping bag and found her breast, she moaned and arched her back to press into his touch.

Adam was on fire, desperate to escape the confines of his sleeping bag, to bring her feminine body into contact with his. He finally had to pull back to fumble with the zipper and wrench it down.

On hearing the sound, Claire froze against him.

"What are we *doing*?"

Hearing the cry of panic, he made himself go still, too. "Claire?"

"I can't!" Her hands fell from his body and she tried to scramble away as much as her sleeping bag would allow.

"Stop." He'd never been in such an agony of desire, but he managed to sound almost calm. "You said no. I heard you. Please don't be afraid of me."

He waited until she said, very softly, "I'm not afraid of you. More…of myself."

His eyes closed as he battled himself. "We kissed, Claire. That's all."

"We…"

Came so close to making love, his body throbbed. But he could stop. She'd made her feelings plain earlier. He hadn't meant for this to happen.

"Let's…try to go back to sleep," he said after a minute. And then, "I don't hear any rain."

"No." She moved, but he couldn't tell if she'd shrugged, hunched, what. "Okay." After a pause, she added, "I'm—"

He interrupted, "Don't even think about saying you're sorry."

Chapter Thirteen

It was still dark when Claire woke up, and she guessed immediately that Adam had moved, or his breathing had changed, or something. With her head resting on his shoulder, her forehead pressed to the side of his neck, she was in a position to know. The rest of her… Yep, she'd managed to squirm partway on top of him, only the bulk of two sleeping bags thwarting her.

She tried to ease herself back, but discovered his arm wrapped her and his hand spanned her waist. When he felt her resistance, he lowered the arm. He must have been cold, having much of his chest, shoulder and arm outside the sleeping bag, but it appeared she hadn't given him much choice.

"Let me check the time," he murmured. "Close your eyes."

She did as he asked, but she still saw stars when he turned on the flashlight.

"Three forty-five. Up and at 'em." His satisfaction was plain. Apparently, he *could* set an internal alarm.

Too bad she felt no enthusiasm at all for shedding the sleeping bag and getting dressed, never mind launching in the near dark. But he was right—even an hour lead on their pursuers might allow them to reach the narrow channel unseen, especially if they could be well on their way before full sunrise just after five o'clock.

"Ugh," she mumbled, and got herself into action.

The rain had definitely stopped, and when they pushed their way to the shore and Adam shone the flashlight toward the water, it appeared less choppy than yesterday.

Neither said another word until they sat hunched over their bowls of oatmeal. Then she asked, "How's your shoulder today?"

As if it hadn't occurred to him to wonder, he rotated his arm. "Good," he said, sounding surprised. "A lot better."

She only nodded. Being that the sky hadn't begun even to subtly lighten, he probably didn't see her.

"Last night," Adam said abruptly. "I want you to know I didn't plan that. You don't have to be afraid."

"Apparently I'm not," she said dryly. "I practically climbed on top of you to get comfy."

"I noticed." A smile could be heard in his voice.

"Anyway." Claire was determined to be fair. "It's not like I wasn't...participating."

"I noticed that, too."

"I'm not sure I'd have thought of birth control, and I'm not on any, so it's a good thing we stopped."

"I have condoms," he said.

"*What?* How could you?" He hadn't even had a wallet when she rescued him!

Adam interrupted, "Kyle. I found them in his toiletry bag."

Her mouth opened and closed a few times as if she were a fish. Had Adam had her in mind when he decided to hold on to the condoms? Or was it just a waste-not, want-not thing?

She knew better than that, but wasn't prepared to think about it right now. So she said briskly, "Let's just put what happened behind us. Are you done eating? I'll wash up the dishes if you'll roll the sleeping bags and mats."

Without comment, Adam rose.

Did he have the condoms in his pocket *right now*?

No, no. Not thinking about it.

The packing up went so smoothly, she was forced to realize how adept he'd become at everything but the kind of maneuvers in the kayak and strokes she hoped he wouldn't be called on to perform.

Let this work.

The hardest part was carrying the kayaks and gear across the wet, slimy slabs of rock to the water. No waiting for daylight and the turn of the tide for them. Even with each using a flashlight to allow them to see where to put their feet, they both skidded a few times, and once Adam swore.

"Did you hurt yourself?"

"Stepped in a damn tide pool."

"Oh. I hope you didn't—" Claire cut herself off before she could make him feel guilty if he'd smashed a sea urchin or star or... She rolled her eyes and ordered herself to get her priorities straight.

It didn't take them long to load their kayaks. They'd used enough drinking water that both would be a little lighter.

After lowering herself into the cockpit and snapping the spray skirt into place, she used the paddle to nudge herself forward and into a long glide. Moments later, Adam joined her.

Only a few minutes later, he said, "The tide is still coming in, isn't it?"

"I'm afraid so." Slack was best, when the tide was hesitating before changing direction. "Since we can't wait, this morning we'll be paddling against it for a couple of hours unless we want it to carry us back down the channel."

"I'd like us to hug this side of the island for a little ways before we start across," he said. "We might spot their camp."

Alarm leaped in her as if he'd stamped down on a gas pedal. "The idea is to avoid them."

"I'd be happier to sabotage their boat."

Adam sounded so reasonable, as if his suggestion was matter-of-fact. As it probably was for him. If *he'd* been the healthy one and an expert kayaker, *he* wouldn't have hesitated to leave her and strike out on his own. She had the appalling realization that what to her was extraordinary or terrifying was his normal.

"I *hate* that idea."

"If we do see their boat, I don't expect you to come with me. In fact, all you should do is loiter somewhere you can hide if worse comes to worst—"

If he was killed.

"Or join me when I appear again."

"May I remind you that it's still dark and we need to stay well off the shore so we don't split open the hull of one of our kayaks on a big rock?"

"Let's just stay close enough to spot a kerosene lantern or a flashlight. Or an obvious inlet or beach."

Claire swallowed further arguments. She'd expressed her feelings about this stupid idea, but wasn't entirely sure he'd follow her if she ignored him and struck out directly east.

As she turned to go northeast along the coastline, her stomach churned. If she'd known what he had in mind, she wouldn't have eaten the oatmeal that now felt like a load of sand in her stomach.

THIS WAS STUPID. Claire was right, damn it. They needed to use the darkness to run, not go on the attack.

Adam recognized his problem. He craved the feeling of control. Needed to take action, not to continue as a passive victim.

A flicker of light caught his eye.

He pointed to it with his paddle, hoping Claire would see.

She'd quit paddling. Oh, yeah, she saw.

Adam edged his kayak to come up beside hers. "I want to take a closer look. I won't go ashore. You're right—it's too risky. But we could get really lucky and find this is some other kayakers who could call for help."

"Oh! Yes."

He led this time, trying to ensure his paddle slipped quietly in and out of the water without a splash. The campsite, if that's what this was, came closer with startling speed.

The tide going in, the pull carrying them toward the shore. He had to watch it.

At that thought, he quit paddling and reached for the binoculars he'd hung around his neck. Through them, he saw the light brighten. Someone was turning up a lantern. In that flare, he spotted a bulky shape between the light and the water.

Adam swore under his breath. "It's them. We need to get out of here."

This time, she took the lead, taking a rounded turn. Sometime in the next hour, they'd see the sun rise directly in front of them.

They hadn't been underway ten minutes when he heard a motor coming from the north. Circling the island, maybe? Strange, this early in the morning. Then he heard it cough, unlike the smooth running of the newer outboard motor on the inflatable. Was this the aluminum skiff, joining up Boyden and Gibbons? Say, to plan a pincer scheme intended to crack him and Claire like a walnut in a nutcracker? Or maybe only to split up with the idea of blocking more options they might have for escape?

Didn't matter.

Adam cursed himself for delaying their crossing even by the fifteen minutes or so they'd lost.

Thank God they'd left so early.

He fixed his eyes on the darker-on-dark shape of Claire and her kayak, and paddled for all he was worth.

CLAIRE WORRIED THE entire way across. The tug of the current trying to pull them south kept them working hard, but that wasn't all. Out toward the middle of the channel, choppy waves got rougher, then became whitecaps and even minor swells. She was terrified of losing sight of Adam, but he did well sticking close to her stern.

At one point she was sure she heard an outboard motor again, although it was impossible to pinpoint from which direction. How much experience did their pursuers have in rough conditions, or boating at all? She'd paddled in more dangerous conditions—the day she and Mike had followed the ocean coast of Calvert Island was one—but just because these guys knew how to start a motor and maybe had trawled for fish on a lake a few times didn't mean they wouldn't be scared out here. The swells made it a lot harder for anyone to spot kayakers, too, given their low profile.

As the light grew brighter to the east, Claire almost wished for rain. It would be miserable, but would also make visibility so bad, one of

those boats could pass thirty feet from her and
Adam without seeing them.

No such luck, she saw, as a pale gray sky re-
vealed itself.

Go, go, go.

She kept an eye on her compass, and felt confident that they were heading directly toward the
opening into Spitfire Channel. Unfortunately,
that opening was wide enough that they wouldn't
immediately vanish from sight, as she wished
they could.

The chart had showed an hourglass-shaped
inlet on her port side close to the opening, but
the marks indicated it was usually choked with
kelp. It would be a trap, anyway, with no outlet
but back into the channel. A deeper inlet lay farther along; she felt sure that, even a few weeks
from now, other boats would be anchored in it.
At the moment? She had no idea.

As her mind circled desperately, she cursed
herself for not having made a different choice
early on. Truthfully, this channel slicing between
myriad islands wouldn't let them out *that* close
to where they'd started, but if she hadn't been
so afraid of crossing the deep anchorage east of
their first two campsites, they could have been
hidden in the islands in the Kittyhawk group
until they saw a boat to approach.

Too late.

Keep paddling. Her arms and shoulders ached. She was pushing harder than she had at any time on this trip. After all, she and Mike hadn't been in any particular hurry. Every time she stole a look over her shoulder, though, there was the red-and-orange kayak, Adam paddling as hard as she was. What glimpses she saw of his face showed him to be grimly focused. He wasn't giving away how much pain he had to feel.

The blackish-green hump of Spitfire Island grew ahead and to her right, as did what she knew to be the much larger Hunter Island that formed the northern shore of the Spitfire Channel. Neither looked…hospitable. All she saw was rock and the deep green of impenetrable forest.

The paddling became briefly easier despite the wind-ruffled water and ocean swells. Then, it abruptly became way harder. The tide had turned, and was rushing out of Spitfire Channel.

Their timing couldn't have been worse.

They could *try* ducking into the kelp-choked inlet.

No. Trap, remember?

A jutting finger of Hunter Island suddenly reared to her left, which meant they were entering the narrower channel. She expected the first half of it to be easy to traverse—except, of course, for the battle against the outgoing tide. If only they could reach the neck where it was almost choked off, and only a fathom deep. Tricky for most boats, but both the inflatable and the aluminum skiff would have a shallow draft.

Now, *that*, it occurred to her, would be a good place to set up an ambush—although only if she and Adam could beach the kayaks and be able to set foot on land.

If they could find a place to stop at any time, the two boats hunting them might go right on by.

Yes, but wouldn't it be worse to know the enemy was ahead of them, and could be lying in wait anywhere? Say, setting up an ambush at the narrowest place in the channel?

Keep paddling.

SOMEBODY WAS DRIVING a stake through his shoulder again, and damn, his muscles were screaming. Adam discovered that he'd kidded himself that his workouts kept him in prime condition. He'd barely glanced at rowing machines in his usual gym, and was now thinking twice about that.

He'd studied the charts that Claire had laid out, and hoped like hell she would find a place to stop. He wasn't a quitter, but he didn't think he'd make it all the way through to Kildidt Sound.

This was the toughest paddling yet, with the tide one hundred percent against them. Still, they kept on, and on. He fixed his eyes on Claire and fell into a mind—but not muscle or nerve—numbing rhythm.

The land to each side seemed forbidding. In different circumstances, beautiful, but he wasn't in a mindset to appreciate it.

His relief was huge when they passed the opening for yet another channel, this one going straight south and separating Spitfire Island from Hurricane Island. Claire ignored it, looked over her shoulder at him and passed the wide mouth of what he thought was a dead-end lagoon to their left.

A little later, it looked like Spitfire Channel itself turned directly south. Ahead…he couldn't tell.

This time, Claire turned to follow the densely forested shore. Did she know where she was going?

This coastline wandered. They reached an end, where he was able to lay his paddle across the deck, bend forward and groan.

Claire deftly maneuvered her kayak beside his. He lifted his head to find her looking anxiously at him.

"How are you?" she asked.

"Beat," he admitted, "but I can go on."

"You may have to. I thought we might find a place to put into shore in this lagoon, even if it's only for a break. Otherwise, we'll be going through that narrow bottleneck, and I'd like to do that at slack tide if we can."

"Okay. I haven't heard a motor since we entered the channel."

"No, I haven't, either. The trouble is, they can explore all day looking for us. If we're going to stop, we have to get completely out of sight again."

Why say the obvious?

Because she hadn't seen any possibilities, he assumed.

"We'd better not hang around here," he said.

Claire bit her lip and nodded.

As her kayak shot away from his, he glanced up. Unless he was imagining things, the thin gray cloud cover had darkened. Could be good. Could be very bad. He of all people knew how horrible it was to be drenched and cold, without any way to dry off or get warm.

He thrust his paddle into the water and followed Claire.

To his surprise, she swung suddenly to the right, straight toward a stretch of shore that looked as unwelcoming as all the land had since they launched this morning.

For the first time, he had to skirt a patch of kelp. Strange stuff. The only kelp he'd seen was on beaches, dried or still slimy and stinking. In this quantity, it could be a field blooming with some strange flower.

On the back side of it, Claire must see something, because she kept going. And then he saw it, too: a tiny cove with a gravel beach of sorts. Drift logs were stacked at the back of the beach, the forest looming just beyond. Would it be possible to get over the pile of driftwood?

Claire nosed her kayak onto the gravel and climbed out to pull it higher. His ground to a stop, but he didn't get out.

"I need to explore a little," she said. "Wait here."

Fine by him. Once the spasms in his shoulder relented, he'd stand up. Stretching would be good.

Claire tried to clamber over what appeared to be wet logs, gave up and walked as far left as she could go, then right. After a moment, he lost sight of her.

Adam climbed out of the cockpit so fast, he caught a foot and almost went down. Regaining his balance, he grabbed the forward carrying toggle and hoisted the kayak high enough he could be sure it wouldn't be pulled away by a wave.

By the time he reached the end of the wall of driftwood, Claire popped back out.

"This should work. We'll have to carry the

kayaks farther than usual, but I found a flat spot above the high-tide line."

He reached for her, lifted her off her feet and swung her in a circle. She laughed at him the entire time, until he set her down again, his hands still on her waist.

Adam went for light. "Saving me again." His voice came out gritty, though, and she'd gone solemn, searching his eyes.

He didn't know what she found, but her smile bloomed again.

Her hair had to be stiff with salt spray, her cheeks and nose glowed red, her lips were chapped and all he could think was how beautiful she was.

He was in deep trouble. Had been since that first day when she warmed him so generously with her own body. His cautious nature kept waiting for her to show herself as something less than the foolishly brave, thoughtful, compassionate woman he'd discovered so unexpectedly.

Wasn't going to happen today.

And tomorrow…tomorrow they should make it out to Kildidt Sound, where there had to be other boat traffic.

Beyond that, he couldn't see.

Chapter Fourteen

Late afternoon, Claire stiffened at the sound of an outboard motor.

Adam was already moving, pushing toward the driftwood logs where he could crouch to see through a gap to the small beach. Claire followed and knelt beside him.

"Won't they ever give up?"

He shook his head. "I'm beginning to think they still have the on board. If the yacht owner is unwilling to chance setting up another meet, Dwayne must feel like he's up a creek."

"Without a paddle," she murmured, her eyes fixed on the gray water of the inlet. The brown mat of kelp, rooted on the seabed, bobbed on the rising and falling surface, pulled by the currents. In this backwater, in kayaks they could have cut through it, but Claire was glad they'd been able to find a way around.

"Yeah," Adam agreed in response to her comment, which was almost a pun. But not a funny one. "Bad enough if Dwayne has to go back to Juneau and admit he wasn't able to complete the job, but if he also admits there's a possibility a witness got away, he's a dead man, and he has to know it."

Claire absorbed that. She'd assumed that Adam's sense of urgency had to do with what would happen to the uranium once it reached Seattle, or whatever port at which the yacht had taken refuge. With all the days that had passed now, the door had probably closed to the possibility of keeping the uranium out of the hands of the buyers, whoever they were—unless it was still on the freighter. That would be better for US security, not so good for her and Adam.

"So they never will stop."

His head turned and his eyes met hers. "You didn't ask for any of this. Maybe I should have told you to leave me once I was back on my feet and had the kayak."

"And maybe they'd have shot me if our paths had crossed."

"Your kayak isn't red." He closed his eyes for a moment, his mouth tight. "I don't know. There was no good reason for Dwayne to shoot your friend."

She only nodded. Both of them went back to the too-familiar need to watch for their enemy.

With the sound of the motor growing louder, Adam lifted the binoculars to his eyes.

Almost immediately, he growled an obscenity. "They're across the inlet from us." He handed over the binoculars.

She had to adjust them, but not by much. The inflatable boat came into sharp focus. She'd gotten to hate the sight of it.

"They're searching the shore. How can they possibly know we turned in here and didn't go on through the channel?"

"They don't," he said flatly. "They're being thorough. They know they're faster than we are, and don't want to chance missing us."

She made a small sound that might have been a moan. Adam's big hand gripped her forearm and squeezed.

Claire took a deep breath before she asked, "What do we do if they turn in here on their way back?"

He kept staring, she suspected unseeingly, out at the restless water. The inflatable boat had disappeared from their limited view, although they could still hear it.

Then he said the words she'd dreaded. "Ambush them."

No, HE DIDN'T love the idea of killing Boyden, especially, or even Curt Gibbons. Neither was the sharpest knife in the drawer, and he felt sure they didn't know about that extra cargo. But it was obvious they'd been willing to murder a complete stranger because he was in a kayak that was the right color…and had no qualms about killing Adam when they caught him. What enraged Adam most was that they wouldn't hesitate to also murder the gutsy woman who'd done nothing wrong except save Adam's life.

Maybe their fear of Dwayne drove them, but the hunt had been unrelenting. So, yeah, if he had a chance to knock out either or both, he had to take it.

"Under these circumstances, there's no need to bother disabling the boat," he said. "In fact, we could take it."

"You mean, if…"

He killed the two men. Yeah.

The question was, how could he do that when his only two weapons were a knife and a flare gun?

Knowing they didn't have long, he set Claire up behind the driftwood logs, not far from their camp. He found a solid branch—not driftwood, those were too lightweight—and told her if either of the men made it over the barricade, she should swing for the son of a bitch's head with everything she had.

"Can you do that?" he asked, not sure if her

answer mattered. Even determined people often couldn't pull the trigger when the moment arrived.

She swallowed, firmed her jaw and nodded. She had more steel in her backbone than most people, he'd long since realized. Seeing her good friend shot right in front of her had to be strong motivation, too.

"I'll take one of them out with the flare gun." Depending on whether he could aim it with any accuracy. "And hope I have time to reload it."

He'd practiced during some of their downtime.

If the flare missed… Adam didn't let himself contemplate it for long. Boyden and Gibbons would both be carrying semiautomatic handguns. They'd strafe him with bullets.

His plan was lousy, but if there was a feasible plan B, he couldn't see it. Thinking about leaving Claire on her own felt like a knife blade to his chest.

The sound of the motor had diminished as they talked, but now grew again in volume.

He kissed Claire gently, gazed into her astonishingly blue eyes for a moment that stretched, then turned away to jog to his own hideout.

The wait couldn't have been longer than ten minutes, but felt interminable. His habit was to think of everything that could go wrong and figure out how to shift the odds. Today, the odds were so damn bad, he had trouble envisioning how this could go right—but he'd been in tough places before, and survived.

He'd kept the binoculars with him, but didn't even lift them. When the inflatable appeared, it was so close he could make out the men's faces. They idled on the other side of the field of kelp, Boyden, seated at the stern with the outboard motor, talking and gesturing.

Right then, the motor died.

Some swearing went on, Adam able to hear every agitated word.

Boyden leaned over the back, then gesticulated some more. He raised the rotors from the water, and even Adam was able to see that kelp tangled them, slick and topped by brown bulbs. Meanwhile, the boat bobbed at the mercy of the tide and currents that pushed it farther into the broad bed of kelp.

Adam debated shooting the flare gun at them while they were distracted. The range was farther than he liked, given that he'd never fired the thing. He'd undoubtedly have time to dive back behind drift logs and reload, though.

He kept watching as the two men broke out some oars and clumsily attempted to back out of the trap they were being sucked into. Boyden finally concentrated on cutting the kelp from the propeller, although that left Gibbons to single-handedly wield the oar.

God, what Adam would have given for a gun.

Gradually he relaxed, as what had been impending battle and potential bloodshed became farce. If he hadn't guessed that Claire would find no humor whatsoever in watching those two idiots struggle, he might have enjoyed himself.

He didn't forget that they might yet break free of the field of kelp and decide to take the narrow path free of entanglements to the beach.

Except he noticed something he hadn't earlier. The tide had turned again, leaving wet gravel… and rocks. The kayaks had floated right over them, but they hadn't been exposed then.

No, the beach was no longer accessible. Pray to God those two didn't realize that it ever had been.

PREPARING DINNER A couple of hours later, Claire couldn't help thinking that this could be her last night with Adam. If all went well and they made it the rest of the way through Spitfire Channel tomorrow, they might immediately encounter a boat they could stop. They could be separated from the minute the Canadian Coast Guard responded, or maybe taken to Shearwater or Bella Bella—communities right across the bay from each other—to stay until ferries docked. She would be on one going south, Adam on one going north, or so she assumed.

No, he might stay on a coast guard vessel, it occurred to her.

Not looking at him, she asked, "Are you based out of Alaska?"

He shook his head. "No DEA office in Alaska. I'm currently working out of San Diego. That's where we caught the first whiffs of this particular drug trafficking operation."

"I've never been there."

"It's a nice city. Beaches are great. With the border so close, we're busy."

"I'll bet." She concentrated on dishing up the vegetarian chili she'd served before and that he'd seemed to like. It seemed safest, since she guessed Hurricane Island was plenty large enough to have active wildlife. With the memory of the previous night, Adam hadn't suggested a steak, even tongue in cheek.

"We...tend to get transferred regularly," he commented, after swallowing a bite. "There is a Seattle office."

"Oh." Was he hinting that he might request it? *Sure. Jumping to conclusions, are you?*

"My mom is down in Arizona now," Claire heard herself say. "She likes the dry heat." As if he cared.

"Your father?"

"They're divorced. Did I say that? He's re-married and in South Carolina. He works for Boeing," she added, seeing that he knew the company had a plant there.

"That's why you started at Boeing?" Adam surprised her by asking.

Claire made a face at him. "Of course. Dad knew someone. Once I had experience, I moved on. Boeing is just so huge. Plus, I liked getting a job on my own." She almost tacked on a *You know?* but remembered in time that he'd had no parent to help him get a first job.

"So you've always lived in the Seattle area?"

"Yes. I've sometimes considered venturing farther afield, but... I don't know. The idea is a little scary."

"Scarier than this vacation?" he said with wry humor.

Despite the ache inside, Claire laughed. "My perspective has changed a little."

"On what's fun?"

She loved the smile playing with his lips, but answered seriously. "No, mostly on what I'm capable of doing. I thought I was being brave taking up sea kayaking. Testing myself against nature." She rolled her eyes. "Now I've been stretched beyond anything I thought I could do." She tried to smile, but knew she wasn't successfully. "Like, say, bashing a man's head in with a tree branch."

"I'm glad you didn't have to," he said with sudden intensity. "I hope you never have to do anything like that. Killing a man, even when it's justified, isn't easy to live with."

She scraped the sides of the pan with her spoon by feel, her gaze on his hard face. "These guys are trying to kill *us*."

"They are," he said after a moment. "Even so, I worked with them for over a month. Went out for a beer with one of them. I doubt either had killed before, although I could be wrong about that. They apparently didn't hesitate when they came on Kyle Sheppard, which surprises me. I'd have said they're muscle-on-the-hoof who don't mind breaking the law, but that's not the same as going out on a search-and-destroy mission." He shook his head. "I doubt they know what's really at stake."

Disturbed, she said, "I wanted to hate them."

"I shouldn't have said any of that." He set down his bowl with a sharp movement and reached up with his good hand to knead the back of his neck. "Better you do hate them. I'm afraid now we'll find them lying in wait for us."

"I know." And oh, she didn't want to think about an attack coming out of nowhere. Of straining tomorrow to see anything that didn't fit, listening for the rumble of an outboard motor. Knowing that along most of the way they had yet to paddle, they'd be in a narrow chute between rock shoulders with very few coves shallow enough to offer any chance of letting them get off the water or hide.

If only she'd made a different decision early on, she thought for what had to be the twenty or thirtieth time.

But if she had, they would have been completely exposed in Spider Anchorage. And... could Adam have paddled across that distance the first day they set out? Or even the second day?

She didn't think so. Plus, she didn't believe even Adam had expected a hunt quite so relentless.

"We can't leave until the tide is in," he said out of the blue.

"No. You saw the rocks?"

"Did you know they were there?"

Claire shook her head. "It's actually a miracle one of us didn't scrape our hull."

"What happens if you do?"

She shrugged. "Most often, just a scar. I carry a kit to mend anything more serious, but it's a nuisance."

"Under the circumstances, more than a nuisance," he said dryly.

"One hole won't sink a kayak, any more than it would that raft. Kayaks are designed with bulkheads and multiple air compartments, too, you know."

"Accessed by the different hatches," he murmured in a tone of enlightenment. "I should have realized."

Now she could smile. "Have you been worrying about sinking like a rock?"

His grin changed his face in a way that always startled her, and made her heart do gymnastics. "It's crossed my mind."

"I never thought to ask how well you swim."

"I'm no Michael Phelps, but I can get up and back a few times in the swimming pool. In these waters, does it matter?"

"Well...only to be sure you can hold out until another kayaker comes to your rescue."

He smiled again. "I did that."

"You did." She couldn't help smiling back. But the grin faded when she said, "We can't launch in the dark tomorrow."

"No, I can see why. But early."

Claire nodded. What else was there to say?

RAIN AGAIN, WHICH Adam told himself was a good thing. It gave them a better chance of passing unseen.

Of course, it also limited their visibility, which he hated.

Both he and Claire wore their wet suits and wide-brimmed hats to fend off the rain. Since the rain seemed to be coming down at a slant, the hats weren't as helpful as he'd have liked. At his suggestion, they had also donned rain slickers over, rather than under, their too-bright yellow life vests. With the knife he had taken to carrying, he slit the rain slicker so that he could easily reach the flare gun he again carried in the vest pocket.

They had set out when the sky was barely tinted gray. The tide had just turned, meaning the rocks were once again submerged enough for the kayaks to skim right over them. Paddling out of the inlet was fine, the tide giving them a smooth ride. The moment they turned east, back into the channel, that changed.

Yesterday, he'd seen how narrow it became, but he liked it even less once they were in it. If one boat waited ahead for them, and another came up behind, they were dead.

But how could their pursuers know for sure where they were? Adam had studied the map and charts Claire carried long enough to doubt Boyden and Gibbons could feel any certainty. The waterways were too complex, lace studded with islands and the dark humps of rocky islets. He and Claire could have gone any number of ways. Even using the skiff, too, it wouldn't be possible to watch every route they might have taken.

He especially hoped they weren't watching this one.

His shoulder felt stronger yet today. He wasn't having any trouble keeping up with Claire, even as he searched the shoreline to each side. His gaze lingered on a small cove choked with what had to be kelp, although the veil of rain let him see only a dark mat.

They wound between fingers of rock, abutments that offered no place to beach even if they'd wanted to. Everything around them was painted in shades of gray, from pale to almost black. Wind sighed through the trees and ruffled the water. The rainfall was steady but soft. He had to blink away droplets now and again.

They'd gone a surprising distance, the channel having widened, when it swung south. Claire slowed once and gestured with her paddle toward a cluster of lower rocks on the shore—and the bear and cub both peering into what he guessed were tide pools. Mama swiped a giant paw in one, a silvery fish wriggling from her claws when she pulled the paw out. She flipped it onto the rock slab, then lifted her head and stared at the kayaks.

Adam saw dark shapes in the water that could

have been seals or sea lions a few times—probably too big to be otters, like the one he'd seen close-up the one day. If he hadn't been paddling, he'd have been getting chilled despite the multiple layers he wore, he realized.

Claire stayed in what appeared to be the middle of the channel. Maybe she'd paid more attention than he had to the depth. Stood to reason.

He split from her path to round a small islet, partly to take a better look at what appeared to be a cove or inlet to his right. *Starboard*, he corrected himself. He was about to turn his head to look for Claire when his attention was snagged by a shape that didn't quite fit on what might be a gravel beach, or simply smooth slabs of rock tilting into the water. A pile of snoozing sea lions?

Damn. Could that be the inflatable?

He didn't see any movement around it. Nothing that looked like a tent—but he doubted there'd been a small tent available in the freighter's stores. A little grimly, he hoped Gibbons and Boyden had spent a miserable night huddled under a tarp. If they were lucky enough to have one of those.

He used his paddle to come to a near stop, and waited until Claire reappeared, her head turned anxiously. Then he gestured for her to come closer.

When he pointed, she stared.

"They won't see us going by."

"This is my chance to cripple them. I can beach twenty yards or so away, do some damage to the boat and take off."

For all the sunburn, her face looked pale, her eyes dark in the gray surroundings.

"You hover just past their camp."

"I can help."

Adam shook his head. "If things go wrong, get the hell out of here. Do not put yourself in danger by thinking you can help me."

She nodded.

"We're not far from Kildidt Sound, are we?"

"No. Wait! Even if you slow them down, they must carry a VHF radio, which means they can pinpoint our location."

"That's a downside, but you saw how inadequate the skiff is for any serious pursuit. It ran dangerously low in the water carrying two men. This will give us a jump start."

Adam could tell she wasn't happy, but she dipped her head and said, "Be careful."

He lifted the paddle in a casual response, then dug it in to glide away from her, not letting himself look back. He couldn't be sure whether he was doing the smart thing or not, but if he could eliminate these two, he and Claire might actually have a chance of not only stopping Dwayne and his crew, but also of coming out of this alive.

The alive part wasn't usually something he let himself think much about, but this time…something had shifted in him.

Adam shook his head. He had to get in the frame of mind to do this job and get out. He couldn't afford anything else.

Chapter Fifteen

The sole of Adam's boot skidded on rock that was both wet and slimy with seaweed. Twisting, he barely kept his footing. *Damn, damn, damn.*

He took a moment to regain his composure before gingerly reaching for the carrying toggle at the stern of his kayak and lifting, taking several careful steps until he was sure he had the kayak far enough out of the water that it wouldn't go adrift. It had taken a few minutes to turn it around, but he wanted to be able to jump in and take off with maximum speed.

The flare gun stayed in the vest pocket, but the butt protruded so he could lay his hand on it in an instant. The knife he held in his left hand as he made his way along the shore.

A snort sounded, and he froze. *Not a bear. Please, not a bear.*

But there were no crashing sounds, and nothing moved except overhead branches and the eternal rise and fall of the sea.

At twenty yards he saw lumps beneath a blue tarp. If the sleepers hadn't gotten soaked last night, they were lucky, he thought dispassionately. Hard to be sure, given the rain, but high tide had to have come close to lapping at them. Tying the boat to a tree trunk was smarter than he'd have given them credit for being.

Quiet. Quiet.

He crouched beside the boat and studied what had been left in it. No guns that he could see. He rose to his feet and carefully opened a canvas bag before sticking his arm in it. Almost immediately, he traced the shape of what felt like an aluminum pot. Some energy bars, a jar that might hold...coffee.

Apparently, they'd kept their weapons at their sides.

Okay. He flexed the fingers of his right hand a few times to be sure his grip would be strong, then switched the knife to that hand.

Another snort was followed by a ripple of the tarp. He held his breath. One of the men waking up? Or just rolling over?

If the tide *had* reached them, an unwelcome surprise, they'd have had to stumble up and relocate during the night. No wonder they weren't up with the dawn.

Nothing else happened. The rain kept coming

down. He rolled his shoulders, suspecting Claire had been right. If he slashed the fabric, air would escape with a rush. Probably a loud rush. Too bad the wind wasn't blowing harder—except if it had been, he and Claire might not have been able to launch.

What if he only pierced a few compartments? Would the air seepage be slow enough they'd make it onto the water before the boat began to sink?

Slash, he decided, and make it fast. It would take them a minute to wake up enough to realize what they were hearing and fight their way free from under the tarp.

Slash, and then shoot. He might disable at least one of them.

Adam took a few slow breaths, lifted the knife—and stabbed the blade into the side, wrenching it toward him before yanking it out. Escaping air was as explosive as a whale expelling a breath. He moved fast, gashing, moving a few feet, doing it again.

Shouts came from beneath the tarp as the men thrashed. Looking at the damage he'd done, Adam tucked the knife away and raised the flare gun. Just as one end of the tarp lifted, he fired.

The flare whistled as it sped faster than his eye could follow. Adam didn't wait to see the result, but heard the screams as light flared in an orange-white cascade. He bent over as he jogged away as fast as he dared over the slick rocks.

Vicious profanities reached his ears. Then a shouted, "Beckman? You're dead."

Almost there.

The buzz sounded like a wasp, but he knew better. He dropped almost to his belly for a minute, then threw himself to his feet again. A bullet stung his arm and he reeled before pushing the kayak downward into the water and leaping into the cockpit.

The bow almost submerged but then bounced upward. Adam began to paddle, heading northeast, wanting to put as much distance from the gunman as he could. The sting in his arm became a burn, but he was able to ignore it beyond cursing the fact that the wound was in his good arm. More bullets skimmed over the water too close to the kayak.

Gibbons—he thought that had been his voice—kept shooting until he emptied his magazine. Adam gambled that he was now out of sight and turned gradually to rejoin Claire. He hoped she hadn't panicked, hearing the gunshots.

WHAT IF HE was dead? Oh, dear God.

Claire's fingernails bit into her palms. Her instincts all but screamed at her to go back. To see what had happened. There had to be *something* she could do.

There was. She could follow Adam's instructions. Save the world—or at least some people—from the possibility of a rogue consortium of nutcases with a nuclear bomb.

She couldn't abandon him.

She had to, if he didn't show up soon.

Was that even remotely possible? Considering the number of gunshots she'd heard, how could he be able to get back in his kayak and paddle away?

He can't, she thought in despair, but braced her paddle against the pull of the tide to stay where she was. He hadn't said how long she should wait—and he hadn't thought to give her the watch, anyway—but she didn't dare linger too long, not if he'd failed in his mission. If the inflatable boat was still seaworthy—

Movement through the sheets of rain had her straining to see. She prayed. *Please, please.*

"Claire?" His gritty voice, even kept low, carried.

"Adam?" she whispered. He wouldn't hear her. "Adam?" she repeated.

The bright kayak appeared, altering course until it came straight at her. Claire was terribly afraid tears were running down her cheeks, but she consoled herself he wouldn't be able to tell, as wet as her face was anyway.

He came abreast of her, and laid his paddle across her forward deck where she could grab it. She did the same, the two paddles forming a bridge to turn the side-by-side kayaks into a raft.

"I heard shooting," she managed to say.

"Yeah, I think I got winged." He sounded unconcerned. "They won't be able to follow us."

"You did enough damage to the boat?"

"Yeah."

"What about the men?"

"I think one of them is dead. Badly hurt, at least."

Claire saw grief on his face, grief he was trying to hide. Any tiny bit of reservation about the truth of his original story dissolved in that moment. She was also afraid she fell the rest of the way in love with him.

He continued, "Gibbons probably got burned, but he was in good enough shape to pull the trigger a few times."

A few times. It had sounded like a fusillade to her.

"He recognized me." His eyes met hers from beneath the dripping brim of his hat. "Let's hope the radio was damaged."

Claire swallowed and nodded. She had to do

her best to match his near stoicism. She wouldn't tell him how terrified she'd been when she heard those gunshots.

THEY SEPARATED AND went back to paddling. Claire started worrying about what he'd said about being *winged*. That meant shot, right? In his case, shot *again*. Surely he'd have the sense to suggest a quick stop to bandage his arm if he thought it was seriously bleeding.

The rain let up enough she'd call it a mist. Thank goodness for her spray skirt, mostly keeping water out of her cockpit. Otherwise, she'd be sloshing. She hoped Adam's was working, and that he wouldn't forget the hand-operated bilge pump he carried.

The neoprene booties he wore would keep his feet reasonable comfortable, no matter what, but enough water sloshing around in the cockpit could make its response sluggish.

Maybe another hour on their way, he signaled toward what the generous might call a beach. One that would quickly disappear once the tide started coming back in, Claire realized, but adequate for a quick stop.

A soaking-wet log provided seating once she spread a tarp on it. Adam reluctantly peeled off the rain slicker—which looked as if it had been sliced by a knife on the upper left sleeve—and let her see the bloody garments beneath. No, he wasn't hemorrhaging or anything like that, but when she separated the fabrics, she found a significant gash cut through skin into the muscle.

Peering down at it, he said, "I can ignore it until we stop for the night. Look, it's clotting."

Claire gave him a stern look. "Let me wrap it over your shirt. I'll just cut up an old T instead of digging for the first-aid supplies. But at least it'll be covered. The rain soaking in probably doesn't hurt anything, but the water might be a lot rougher out in Kildidt Sound, and *salt* in an open wound wouldn't feel good."

Looking chastened, he handed over the knife he'd been carrying and waited semipatiently while she cut and ripped until she had a couple of strips of reasonably clean cotton fabric. Once she tied it off, she helped him slide his arm back into the sleeve of the rain slicker.

Then they ate cold foods they had on hand: almonds, dried fruit and granola topped off with candy bars. He swallowed more ibuprofen, restocked from poor Kyle Sheppard's supplies.

The picture of Kyle's body dangling awkwardly over the tree branch flickered in Claire's mind's eye. She did her best to push it back down into whatever recess it had been staying. Forgetting... No, she'd never forget, either the sight of his body or the things they'd had to do to it.

After she and Adam bundled the remains of lunch back into their kayaks, they sat down again. She had an awful disinclination to move. Now that the most immediate enemy had been vanquished, she wanted them to have won. For rescue to be immediately at hand.

She wanted a hot shower, damn it! A real bed. The knowledge that the authorities were on the job, and the threat of nuclear attack was no longer a burden only she and Adam carried.

Instead, gray mist made her feel chilled however warmly she was dressed, and it worried her that Adam didn't look any more excited about getting a move on than she was.

"Are you all right?" she asked at last.

Predictably, he nodded. But then, after a pause, he added, "Wrenched my back a little, and this, uh…"

"GSW?" she supplied tartly, remembering the acronym for a gunshot wound from some mystery or thriller she'd read. Probably one of Mike's.

"Yeah." Adam's eyes smiled more than his mouth did. "Now that we've stopped, my arm has stiffened up some. And the wound does burn."

"There's a shocker."

He laughed. "Are you mad at me?"

Yes! "No. I understand you were doing your

job. Waiting for you, hearing the shots when I knew you didn't have a gun, that was…" Claire found she didn't want to put into words what that had been like. She was too close to doing what she'd sworn she wouldn't.

Any humor on his face had gone, leaving his expression… She couldn't decide. He was troubled, certainly. By the reminder of what he'd had to do? Or because of what, in his view, he'd put her through?

He had to be a remarkably strong man to do a job this hard, one that had to have left him with internal scars to go with the ones on his body. And yet, *he* hadn't hardened so much as to lose his sense of empathy and compassion, felt even for men like their pursuers.

When she studied him again, she saw that he'd taken care of whatever emotion she'd so briefly seen. Sounding brisk, he asked, "You haven't changed your mind about our route?"

"No. This is still our best bet."

They'd discussed this earlier. If they didn't see any boats right away close enough to stop, they'd head southwest across the sound, aiming for Nalau Passage, which they could follow to Fitz Hugh Sound. That being one of the major inside passages, they could wave down a cruise ship or ferry. Claire didn't expect them to get that far, though; Nalau Island and Passage were popular with fishermen. She'd read there were even a couple of lodges aimed at sportfishermen.

Adam nodded. "A nice big fishing boat would suit us just fine."

She made a face. "If I just hadn't dropped my SPOT—"

He gripped her forearm and looked steadily into her eyes. "You had every reason to be shaken by what you'd just seen. Hardly anyone would have had steady hands in the middle of something like that."

"No, but—"

He interrupted her again. "Even the best-planned operations often go off the rails. That's the way it is. You've more than made up for letting the damn thing slip out of your hands by saving my life, and guiding us through these past few days. If you hadn't had the courage to put yourself out there to rescue me, I'd be dead. No question."

"I couldn't just paddle away," she protested.

"No." This smile was crooked, deepening the lines between his nose and mouth, warming his eyes. "You'd never have done that."

He was right, she decided; she'd screwed up the one thing, but done a lot right since then. It was time, once and for all, to ditch the inner critic exacerbated by a desire to head off Devin's constant discontent with her. In fact, she could just plain quit thinking about a guy so inadequate, he had to put other people down to make himself feel better.

Besides, as for her most recent fussing...it wasn't as if she'd had any experience being on the run with a federal agent from murderous smugglers.

"You're smiling."

She grinned at him. "Thank you for making me feel better. Now, I suggest we actually do get our butts back in the kayaks and move on."

Before she could stand, he wrapped her with his newly injured arm, pulled her close and kissed her forehead. She held entirely still, breath caught in her throat, and reveled in the moment.

As he seemed to be doing.

ENERGIZED BY THE hope of being able to contact the coast guard, Adam felt strong enough to go on.

The gray-green bulk of what Claire had informed him was Hurricane Island reared ahead. Tiny, tree-topped lumps of rock appeared from the mist. None were big enough to qualify as islands. This whole area was a maze.

As she'd warned him, the more open the water, the more it felt like real ocean, swells replacing swirls of currents. He was able to keep her in sight, and the waves weren't large enough to challenge his limited kayaking skills, but he was having to work harder. The new injury had progressed from burning to a deep ache that felt as if the bone had been cracked. He knew that wasn't so, but muscles and ligaments in his upper arm *were* attached to the humerus, the long bone. And some of them had to be damaged.

The older, more serious wound had woken up in the last hour, too. This pain was deep in his shoulder and torso, and diffuse. Nothing he couldn't ignore, but he'd really like to see a gill-netting fishing boat any minute.

Like now.

A curiously even line of those islets, these bigger than some, stretched ahead, north to south. Claire was staying well away from them, and something about the turmoil of the surrounding seas made him wonder if there weren't more rocks that lurked just beneath the water.

Adam had been studying the islets, but he heard something that snapped his attention back to Claire.

She'd come to a virtual stop, and was trying to turn around, sliding sideways on a long swell. What the hell…?

The bulk of a ship appeared against the gray seas. The silhouette wasn't one Adam had ever wanted to see again, unless he was in a helicopter with a dozen members of the Canadian Coast Guard or Navy. He reached for the binoculars and, despite the droplets that immediately blurred the lenses, confirmed his fear.

That rusty old tub was sitting out here waiting for them.

Chapter Sixteen

If anyone aboard the freighter was standing watch, it would be hard to miss the two kayakers heading straight for them. Especially him in this electric-orange-and-red kayak.

He struggled to turn, too, just as Claire reached him.

"Do you see it?" she called. "Is it them?"

"Yes," he roared, "and let's get the hell out of here."

"If we can drop behind the Mosquito Islets—"

"Damn it." He'd been craning his neck. "They're doing something." Then he knew. "Lowering the skiff down to the water."

The skiff wasn't much, but it did have an outboard motor. Even a single man in it could strafe them with bullets.

At that moment, the sound of an engine reached him, throaty and deep. Multiple engines. He turned his head sharply and saw a snow-white sharp-prowed boat cutting in front of them not half a mile ahead. Thirty to forty feet long, maybe, with a big cabin and what might be radar equipment topside. He'd seen plenty of sportfishing boats like this when he'd been based in Miami.

What scared Adam was wondering whether Dwayne and company would think twice about killing half a dozen more people.

He took a hand from the paddle to pull out the flare gun. Adam closed his eyes, but only for an instant.

This was a risk, but what choice did they have?

He pointed the gun at the sky and pulled the trigger.

Not thirty seconds later, the flare shot high into the air, a vivid, sparkling, universal call for help. Damn. Had the fishing boat gone far enough past them, people in the cabin wouldn't have seen the flare? He fumbled for the plastic bottle that held more flares and extracted one to reload, but first he twisted to look back. If the skiff was in the water, he couldn't see it, no surprise considering it was aluminum against the gray-on-gray landscape.

He pivoted back to see the fishing boat slowing, beginning a turn. Kicking up waves of its own and a frothing white wake. After shoving the flare gun into his PFD pocket, he dug in his paddle, saw Claire doing the same and wished they were in the US where there might have been a chance in hell one of the boaters would be armed.

He started paddling again, Claire doing the same. God help them, they couldn't outrun any boat with a motor, but the much larger fishing boat approached them a lot faster than the skiff could.

A putt-putt behind them reached his ears. Adam didn't bother looking back. A shot. The sportfishing boat closed the distance. A quarter mile, a few hundred yards. He pinned his gaze on it, paddling for all he was worth even as he veered to fall in behind Claire. Maybe the shooter would be content to kill him and would let her go. Or maybe, paddling just a little bit ahead, she'd be able to slide out of sight behind the larger boat in time.

People crouched on the narrow walkway at the prow, waving and calling, although he couldn't hear what they were saying. A man midway back had binoculars trained on something beyond the kayaks.

Water kicked up less than a foot from the port side of Adam's hull. The muffled crack of a rifle shot came after it. He had a minute then while he slid down the back side of a swell high enough to hide him.

One of the men in the boat ahead bellowed

through a bullhorn. "Stop firing a gun! We've called for the coast guard. You're committing a crime—"

Adam's kayak jerked sideways. It had been hit.

Afraid you'll sink like a rock? Claire had asked.

Here was his chance to find out what really would happen.

The next thin line of water shooting above the waves was close to Claire's kayak. Damn. The men on board the sportfishing boat were retreating from the prow and railing, alarm evidence.

Then one of them shouted and pointed. Adam couldn't see what they did, but a moment later a new flare shot into the air. Claire's kayak sped by the prow of their rescuers and tucked in behind it. Adam fought to keep his kayak lurching ahead.

Another shot, another. A spray of bullets surrounded him. One could have struck him, and Adam wasn't sure if he'd have noticed. He saw a man on the fishing boat drop out of sight suddenly.

But then another, similar boat approached, and Adam saw a third one speeding toward them from the south. Every skipper who'd seen the flare was responding.

He bumped into the side of the first boat, his

hull scraping it. Nobody reached down toward him or hung over the thwarts, but the next thing he heard was music to his ears.

"It's turning around! It's running away!"

With a groan, Adam slumped forward, head almost touching the deck. The kayak was still gliding forward—until a paddle was thrust toward him and he was able to grab it. Claire held firm until the two kayaks once again lay side by side, and he could clumsily hold an arm out to her.

He thought she said, "We made it."

"ONCE WE SAW that someone was shooting, we called for the coast guard," said the red-faced man who looked like a former football player who was thickening around the middle.

Adam asked, "Did one of you get shot?"

"Tony Vargas." The guy jerked his head toward what appeared to be the steps leading down to the cabin. "We moved him right away." His expression was grim, as were those of the four other men surrounding them. "What the hell is this about?"

They'd hauled Claire and Adam as well as their kayaks up onto the first boat. The other, similar boats stayed close.

Claire asked anxiously, "Is he badly hurt?"

"Not good. Gut shot," one of the men said.

She saw Adam and that man lock gazes for a moment, but couldn't know what they shared.

Beside her, Adam exhaled a long breath. "Long story. Are you Americans or Canadians?"

"American." That was the first speaker. He nodded toward the boat closest to them. "They're Canadians. I think the others are Americans, too. They're putting up at the same camp we are."

"I'm Claire Holland," she offered. "From Seattle. I was…sea kayaking with a friend when all of this started. He was shot…"

"Adam Taylor. I'm with the US Drug Enforcement Administration. Things went wrong during an operation. I was undercover with drug smugglers." He hesitated. "Some of what happened, and that I know, needs to wait for the coast guard. But the immediate story is that Claire and her friend chanced on the ship I was on while it was transferring illegal cargo."

He told the bare bones of the story: her dead friend, getting shot himself, her rescue, their discovery that they were being hunted.

She gestured north. "We popped out of the Spitfire Channel to find the freighter that was carrying the drugs anchored where they saw us immediately. They lowered a skiff into the water and that's what was pursuing us."

"We're sitting in deep water," one of the men

said uneasily. "Any chance this freighter will show up any minute?"

She saw the expression on Adam's face just before he donned his mask, something he did so well. Yes, he thought that was conceivable.

What he said was, "I doubt it. Three boats here, others that will come running if we shoot off another flare. They have to know at this point that someone will already have been in contact with the authorities. The smartest thing they can do is run. What I don't know is whether they'll continue south or go back north to Alaska. I want that ship boarded before it can dock."

The apparent skipper on this boat had been listening from the doorway into the wheelhouse. Now he nodded toward something behind him— probably a radio. "Sounds like the coast guard cutter will be here in fifteen, twenty minutes. They were tied up at Shearwater. A helicopter is on the way, too. Vargas needs to get medical care fast."

Claire, for one, would be very glad when that coast guard ship appeared. Right now, she felt dazed. Was this even real? Believing she and Adam had actually made it, that they would survive, didn't come easily.

Reassurance came from the rocking motion of the boat bobbing on the waves, and from her feeling so chilled. And the sight of Adam, dirty, wearing a week-old beard that didn't quite hide the furrows on his face that were so much more deeply carved than they'd been the first time she saw him.

He kept glancing at her, checking to be sure she was okay the same way she was doing with him. The minute she'd been helped to a seat, he'd chosen the one beside her. Their arms brushed. She needed to stay connected to him.

And how long will that last? she asked herself. She already knew the answer. Not for long.

Authorities would want to hear her description of events. After that, their next concern would be figuring out how to get her home. But Adam, he'd have to keep doing his job. Their closeness felt more real than anything else that was happening, but it was the illusion, not these kind men surrounding them. Or the *whap whap* of helicopter rotors she heard.

They all turned their heads, looked up. A red-and-white-painted helicopter swooped toward them. Several of the men on this boat stood and waved their arms over their heads.

Within minutes, a medic had dropped down to the boat deck from the helicopter, bringing a stretcher with him. With the help of a couple of the fishermen, Tony Vargas was strapped to the stretcher. He was in so much pain, Claire wanted to look away from his face but didn't let herself. He was another victim of these monstrous criminals, just as Mike had been, and then Kyle Sheppard.

Oh, God, she thought. If she didn't have cell phone coverage, she could surely borrow a VHF radio to call Shelby and tell her Mike was dead.

She'd never had to bring that kind of news to anyone, and didn't want to start now. But it had to be her, not some impersonal police officer asked to do the notification by Canadian authorities.

"What are you thinking?" Adam asked, as the stretcher swung into the air, being winched to the open door of the helicopter hovering above.

"That I should call Mike's wife."

He took her hand in his, the warmth more comforting than it should have been. "Why don't you wait until we talk to the people from the coast guard? We don't want your friend's wife—"

"Shelby."

He nodded. "Shelby calling friends or family to tell them, or posting what she knows about his death on social media, until investigators are ready to release the information."

She wriggled her hand, but he didn't release it. "You mean, you?" Claire asked.

"I'm one of them." His expression was gentle,

his voice less so. "Most of it will be taken out of my hands from here on out."

"I'm glad." Seeing his raised eyebrows, Claire said, "You need to go to a hospital and have your wounds checked out."

A smile appearing in his eyes, he rotated his right arm. "Now you're telling me you didn't know what you were doing when you patched me up?"

She wrinkled her nose. "You know I didn't."

He dipped his head toward her, speaking too softly for any of the other men to hear. "I think you did." His breath tickled her ear. "Turns out, you're a lot more capable than you knew you were."

After a moment, she straightened. He was right. She'd proved herself over and over this week. The challenge she'd believed she and Mike were facing was nothing in comparison. She'd have gone home feeling good about their adventure, but now...

I'm more than I knew I was.

But she couldn't forget the cost. She'd miss Mike, although that was nothing to what Shelby would have to endure. Kyle Sheppard must have had friends and family who would be plunged into shock and grief. Tony Vargas, another vacationer, might not survive.

And Claire knew life would never seem the

same to her. How could she have fallen so hard for a man in a matter of days? Dread filled her at the idea of saying goodbye and going home.

It was like having a huge hollow opening inside her. She might have even made a sound, because Adam said, "What?"

"I... Nothing." His gaze on her face was keen enough, she could tell he wasn't satisfied. "I'm feeling too much. I mean, we started today with your raid on that encampment, we paddled hard in the pouring rain only to face new disaster, we saw the hope of rescue that might not happen because of the bullets flying, and now here we are."

"Yeah," he said gruffly. His arm came around her. "These last days, you've been a constant in my life I've never had."

"There's the coast guard lifeboat!" a man at the rail called, interrupting them.

A lifeboat? That sounded...puny.

"Finally," Adam murmured.

HALF AN HOUR LATER, the two of them were aboard a ship that might have been fifty feet long. It was painted in an eye-catching bright red and white, which Adam knew to be the Canadian Coast Guard colors. Their kayaks and all their possessions had been transferred, too.

He'd shaken hands with everyone on the sportfishing boat, and a few who leaned across from one of the other boats. Claire hugged everyone, sniffled and then mumbled to him during the transfer, "I probably stink!"

Adam laughed. "I'm sure I do, too. And I can guarantee that nobody cares."

The ship carried a crew of five officers and four others. Six men, three women. Several of them studied the bullet hole in the red kayak before two officers led him and Claire to a cabin to talk.

They listened to his recitation of events, called the number he gave them for confirmation of who and what he said he was and let him speak to his immediate superior.

"We were just starting to get seriously worried about you. I know you expected that tub to turn around and go back to Juneau, but it hasn't docked. Tell me again where you are?"

Adam gave him the bare bones, too, to which the two Canadians listened closely. Then he said, "That freighter *has* to be stopped before it docks or has a chance to transfer cargo. That's got to be a number one priority for both governments. Some or most of the drugs have already been handed off." He gave the identifying details on the yacht. "However, we were interrupted before we were done. That's when the first kayaker, Mike Maguire, was shot and killed, and when I was shot and went overboard." Adam glanced at the two coast guard officers and gave a mental shrug. "They were transporting something else, too. I...overheard the head guy, Dwayne Peterson, talking to his number two man. They'd been paid a lot of money to pass along a little extra."

Everyone in the cabin stayed so quiet, he couldn't hear them breathing. Even Russ Garman, his supervisor, only waited.

"Uranium," Adam said.

Even Claire blinked at the urgency of ensuing conversations. What she took for an oceangoing version of the order, be on the lookout, went out to other coast guard vehicles as well as Canadian ferries and, who knew, Canadian naval vessels? She sat, quiet and forgotten, as US naval and coast guard people were patched into conversations with their Canadian counterparts.

One of the officers left the cabin, and minutes later she realized that the small ship was underway. Taking her and maybe Adam to a drop-off point? Or searching for the freighter that had—what?—an hour head start on them?

Searching, apparently, although it eventually occurred to somebody to feed her and Adam, after which she was escorted to pick up her toiletries and clothes from her kayak before being left in what she felt sure was one of the senior officers' cabins. The shower was tiny but functional. Washing her hair and shaving made her feel amazing. Finally, she dressed in clothes she always held back for the days she and Mike planned to spend a night in civilization—i.e. someplace with showers and real beds.

Then she wiped the steam from the mirror and eyed herself. What she saw wasn't as heartening as she'd hoped. Her sunburn was cycling through a couple of stages at the same time: fiery red and peeling. Her lips were cracked. As she'd seen with Adam, her face looked almost...gaunt.

She slathered her face with cream, rubbed her lips with an ointment and called it good. At least she *felt* better.

When she reappeared on the deck, she didn't find Adam. A female crew member smiled at her and said, "Your partner is showering. He should be out soon."

Claire wandered to the rail. The small ship was moving fast, and when she scanned the closest land, she thought they might be heading north toward Princess Royal Island. Was the plan to leave her off at Klemtu instead of Bella Bella or Shearwater? But she suspected no one was thinking about her. They were searching for the rusty, decades-old freighter she'd really, really prefer never to see again.

Wind whipped through her hair. Trying to corral it with one hand, she shivered and decided to go back to the borrowed cabin and add another layer or two for warmth. And maybe braid her hair.

But just as she started to turn, an arm came around her. Startled, she looked up at Adam's face.

"You shaved," she blurted.

He laughed. "I do that now and again." He studied her. "You're still sunburned."

Scrunching up her nose hurt the tender skin, but she did it anyway. "Gee, I didn't notice."

A smile lingered at the corners of his lips, but he didn't say anything else, only tucking her close to him for warmth, serving as a wind block.

After a few minutes, she couldn't resist asking. "What did I miss?"

"Not much. We've spread our net along the US border both to the north and south. Coast guard and other vessels are watching for the freighter out here in Queen Charlotte Sound and Hecate Strait, and in the passages and channels that make up the inside passage. Some helicopters and small planes are in the air, too."

"And we're out here looking for it, too."

"Yeah," he said slowly. "Part of me doesn't want to hand over the hunt, but the other part..." He hesitated.

She made sure he held her gaze when she asked the question that had been bothering her from the minute she realized the coast guard lifeboat wasn't puttering back to dock in Shearwater again.

"What if we *do* see it? I mean, except for us there are only nine people aboard. And…this is Canada. How well armed are their coast guard personnel? What kind of weapons do your former shipmates carry?" She bit her lip. "If we see the freighter and try to stop it, isn't that kind of suicidal?"

Chapter Seventeen

Adam admitted to sharing her reservations. That said, he doubted they'd be the ones to find the freighter. He hoped not; he'd be a lot happier if Dwayne and company were taken into custody by US authorities, rather than him having to take on the extradition hassle, or allow the Canadians to prosecute the traffickers.

In fact, the coast guard lifeboat had been underway not much over an hour when he was told it was turning around, thanks to a desperate call from a capsized sailboat. They were the closest help to hand.

This was going to be a seriously crowded vessel by the time they reached a port.

He and Claire were allowed to join the captain to listen in on radio discussions concerning his target. The second officer was handling their response to the immediate crisis.

There was a time when Adam would have itched to be part of the boarding operation. Personally slapping the cuffs on Dwayne. Strangely, he felt a sense of distance instead. He was interested, and intensely focused on finding out whether the uranium was still on board and could be seized. But he'd been changed by the events of this week. By the remarkable woman to whom he owed his life.

He'd wanted her from the first night. Now that the desperate need to protect her had relented, he was free to concentrate on how he'd ask her to share a bed tonight.

Surely, wherever they were, there would be a bed.

But he wanted more than that, and hated not knowing whether she felt the same. Sometime in the past forty-eight hours, he'd been slammed with the full understanding of what he was prepared to do to keep her. Would she even consider committing herself to a man like him, a man who had no experience with family or long-term promises made on a personal level?

Feeling a little sick, missing whatever was being said over the radio, he asked himself why she *would* pick someone like him. Underneath the sunburn was a sweet face. Combine that with her curvy body, she must frequently have men hitting on her. Adam liked her pretty blue eyes, her smile and light blond hair, too, but he especially liked her smarts, her competence and the empathy that had her hurting after the two deaths they'd seen directly. What made him think the word *love* for the first time in his life, though, was her courage and her sheer grittiness. He could trust her never to let him down—if she loved him in turn.

Right now, she sat as close beside him as she could without drawing notice. In fact…he reached over under the table for her hand, and felt better right away when she returned his clasp.

Once they located the sailboat, lying on its side in increasingly rough water, Adam and Claire stayed out of the way but watched the efficiency of this rescue. The man and woman clinging to the boat, mostly staying out of the water but having waves washing over them, were brought aboard. Emergency efforts to warm them were begun immediately.

When one of the rescuers repeatedly asked whether they had been the only two people on the boat, the man managed to nod. The tension level dropped considerably.

The man was in bad shape, clearly dazed and confused about where he was, shuddering, teeth chattering, what few words he summoned slurred. Recognizing all the symptoms, Adam felt as if cold fingers were walking up his spine.

The woman, though, was almost completely

unresponsive. He'd been there, too. It was a miracle she'd been able to hold on to the capsized boat as long as she had. The decision was made to call for the helicopter again. In the meantime, the captain let Adam know they were heading for Bella Bella, where there was a small hospital.

"Good cell phone service," he added. "Air field, too," he told Adam. "If you'd prefer to fly out rather than taking the ferry."

"I assume we can find someplace to spend the night?" he asked.

"We'll transfer you to Shearwater once we unload our patient. It's better set up for visitors."

"I don't want to go anywhere until I know that damn freighter has been stopped."

The captain's expression held answering grimness. "That may come before we dock."

Ten minutes later, it did.

A US naval ship closed fast on the freighter from the moment it was spotted from the air. One fear had been that Dwayne would decide to dump the especially incriminating cargo overboard, potentially poisoning the ocean, but that hadn't happened. His crew was so obviously outgunned, they'd surrendered without a fight, although the naval officer reporting said, "First thing out of Peterson's mouth was, *This is all that damn Rick Beckman's fault.*" Humor entered the voice. "He was even unhappier when we informed him that Rick Beckman was an alias for a United States federal law enforcement agent."

Adam leaned forward. "The uranium?"

"Recovered, Agent Taylor. You have done a great service to two countries."

His fingers tightened on Claire's hand when he said honestly, "The one we really owe is the woman who saved my life and kept me a step ahead of Peterson's killers."

"Is she with you, Agent Taylor?"

"Right here." Adam squeezed her hand.

"Ms. Holland, I regret not having the chance to meet you and thank you in person. I would hope you'd be awarded a medal by our government, except—"

Adam was meant to interrupt with a hard truth. "That won't happen. This is the kind of operation that will be buried in a deep, dark hole."

"I assumed as much."

He signed off. The coast guard captain stood, bending his head at her. "I agree entirely, Ms. Holland." Then he quietly left the two of them alone.

Adam turned to face Claire. "You deserve a Presidential Medal of Freedom."

She smiled at him. "Thank you, but I don't want one. I just want—" Looking appalled, she screeched to a stop.

"You want?" he echoed softly.

"For those creeps to all spend a long time in jail." Her eyes widened even more. "Did you tell them about—what did you say his name is?"

"Curt Gibbons. Yes. I feel sure he's been retrieved by now, assuming he hadn't somehow gotten that boat mended enough to put it in the water." He smiled, and not nicely. "Of course, his mother ship abandoned him, which must have come as a shock."

Claire nodded, but not as if she'd been paying that much attention to what he was saying.

"This really is all over."

"It is."

"I don't suppose anyone has found Mike's body."

"Under the circumstances, I think we'd have been told."

"Yes. Um. Will you head back to San Diego? Or up to Alaska?"

It was hard to say, *I do have to keep doing my job, but I'd like to start something with you, too. See where it goes.* The words stuck in his throat, so he said only, "I'm guessing Alaska for the short term. This is my investigation."

"Then tomorrow will be goodbye." She aimed a smile his direction that looked fake, shot to her feet and was out the door and onto the open deck before he could react.

IT WAS JUST as well they weren't alone together again until they'd docked first at Bella Bella, where she and Adam had walked to the Royal Canadian Mounted Police station. There, they left Kyle Sheppard's wallet, passport, locked cell phone and a few other items that seemed personal. The officer had been in contact with the coast guard and expected them; the coast guard had the instructions for where to find Kyle's body for recovery. It would be up to some lucky RCMP officer to notify Kyle's family about his death. Both Adam and Claire passed on their phone numbers in case anyone close to Kyle had questions.

It didn't take long to cross the bay to Shearwater, also clinging to the water's edge, where they left their kayaks in a designated area. The goodbyes with the coast guard officers and crew were as heartfelt as those with the sportfishermen had been.

Walking down the dock away from the big boat, carrying a bag with clothes and toiletries, Claire felt dazed anew. So many people who'd become so important to her in such a short time.

The courage and kindness extended to them had renewed some of her lost faith in her fellow humans.

She couldn't tell whether Adam felt the same; he must have had many such experiences during his career. Maybe, after his unrooted upbringing, he lacked any ability to make deep connections with other people. That thought was unutterably depressing.

He'd been on the phone almost nonstop the past hour or two, and Claire had taken some of that time to call Shelby. Only later, when she lifted her head to savor irresistible smells from a nearby restaurant did he tuck the phone in a pocket. They walked into the restaurant, Claire expecting them to draw stares, but they weren't the only outsiders here today. A hot meal she hadn't had to prepare on her tiny, one-burner cookstove might as well have been gourmet, as far as her taste buds went. Adam inhaled his meal, too, and they each had a slice of pie besides.

The waitress gave them directions to a hotel. Even if the sun was still high in the sky, Claire felt as if this day had gone on for an eternity.

Adam looked preoccupied as they walked. They'd almost reached the place when he said suddenly, "We going to share a sleeping bag tonight?"

A quiver deep in her belly shook Claire. She faltered in her next step forward. Hadn't she expected this moment to come? This decision? But it really wasn't one at all.

"I think we can share tonight." Wow, she'd

almost sounded faintly amused, even sophisticated.

The tilt of his mouth told her "almost" pretty much said it all.

Adam grabbed her hand and hustled her inside. The smiling proprietor led them to his "best" room, small but adequate and including a private bath with a shower. The moment she left them alone, Adam dropped his bag on the floor, took Claire's from her and tossed it on the only chair and gripped her shoulders.

Voice filled with gravel, he said, "God, I want you."

In answer, she went on tiptoe and flung her arms around his neck.

Then his mouth on hers ended all doubts, all possibility of second thoughts. He ate at her mouth, his tongue insistent, the bite of his fingers part of the fierce need she'd seen in his eyes. He groaned when he tore his mouth from hers to nip her earlobe and move damply down her throat. His teeth closed for a not-quite-painful moment on the muscle that ran from her neck to her shoulder. Then he grabbed the hem of her fleece top and wrenched it up, pulled it over her head.

Claire cooperated fully even as she did battle with *his* clothes. She had a fleeting memory of the one time she'd seen him entirely naked, never imagining they'd get to this point. Photos in celebrity magazines were as close as she'd ever come to seeing a man with his kind of body: broad shoulders, long, powerful muscles in his arms, chest and legs. Dark hair that made the sight even more tempting.

And then there was his erection. That had *zero* resemblance to what she'd so briefly seen when she was trying to bring him back from near death.

They all but fell onto the bed, Adam's weight on her, his penis nudging at her opening already. She was so, so ready…but caution was built into her nature.

"Wait! I'm not on birth control. Did you hold on to those condoms?"

He stayed suspended above her for an instant, gaze hungry and intense, before he made a ragged sound and rolled off her.

"Yeah."

To her dismay, he had to get off the bed and crouch by his bag to dig inside it. When he came back to the bed, he had a handful of packets that he let fall onto the scarred bedside stand. But one he ripped open, and with shocking speed he'd spread her legs and thrust inside her.

The sex was hard and fast. Claire had never felt anything like this. It was like being swept up by a hurricane compared to a mild breeze that might ruffle her hair.

After the shattering finale, she had one glimpse of his face before he removed his weight from her and tucked her close, her head on his shoulder. Unless she was imagining things, he looked as shaken as she felt. Maybe just because their past week had been so intense, she told herself. Both of them had built up so much tension, fear and occasional triumph and, yes, sexual tension, it had to be released somehow.

Letting him go without weighing him down with her feelings and regret would be the single hardest thing she'd ever done.

NOT FIVE MINUTES LATER, Adam's body was already stirring. He had every intention of making love with Claire as many times as they could manage tonight. But first he wanted to revel in how she felt in his arms. The hair he rubbed his cheek against was silky, smelling faintly of some unknown shampoo, but underneath he recognized her scent. She fit perfectly against him, which he had already realized after their nights in a shared sleeping bag. Adam hated knowing they had to part ways tomorrow. He couldn't take her with him, and he couldn't walk out on an operation he hadn't completed. *Fell in love* as an excuse would be on a par with *my dog ate my paperwork.*

Much as he wanted to put off a difficult conversation—what if she said no? Did he get dressed and go out to ask for another room?—he disliked even more the gut-churning fear that had taken up residence in his belly.

So he slid one hand down her back, enjoying the delicate feel of her vertebrae, the inward curve at her waist and the firm feel of her butt, and murmured, "We need to talk."

She stiffened. It was a frightening length of time before she asked, "About what?"

"Us."

He'd never used that word before in this context. Never expected he would.

She pulled away, sat up and grabbed a pillow to cover herself in front. Her eyes searched his. "I need to be able to see you."

Talking about hard stuff to someone who couldn't see you would be easier, Adam felt sure, but he understood why she felt that way. He sat up himself, propping a pillow behind himself so he could lean back against the headboard, and said, "You'll get cold. Wrap the covers around yourself."

She eyed him warily, then did as he'd suggested.

He cleared his throat, although that was unlikely to help. "I want to keep seeing you." That sounded less crazy than, *I want us to spend the rest of our lives together.*

Her lashes fluttered a few times. "How is that even possible, with us separated by a couple of states, and given your job?"

"Once I wrap this operation up, I have plenty of time coming. If you want me to, I'll come to Seattle. I can…get a hotel room if you'd prefer that."

For too long, all she did was study him. Her eyes reminded him of the sea: seemingly clear yet hiding unimaginable depths and currents. "I'd…really like if you came for a visit. Of course you can stay with me."

Visit wasn't quite what he had in mind, but even so, he might have slumped in relief if the headboard hadn't been there for support. "Thank you," he said huskily.

She pressed her lips together. "But…then what?"

He didn't like to hear her sounding timid. That wasn't Claire.

"We haven't known each other a week."

"I know." She smiled weakly. "I shouldn't have even asked that question."

"It was quite a week, though. We got to know each other in a way a lot of people never do."

She waited, her blue eyes fixed on him.

"Then... I'm hoping you might consider re-locating," he admitted. "I can try for a transfer to Seattle, but we tend to get moved regularly. If necessary, I can leave the DEA. But I think I can get a promotion to more of a desk job. If I have you, I want to come home every night."

He was horrified to see tears clinging to her eyelashes. Before he could grovel for assuming too much, if that's what was wrong, Claire flung herself at him. His arms reached out automatically and pulled her in close.

"I was so afraid—" she wailed.

He nuzzled her temple. Fine strands of her hair caught in his evening beard. "Of what?"

"When you said we had to say goodbye—"

"You thought I meant forever?"

Her head bobbed. He felt some dampness against his throat.

"I've never felt like this before." He had to swallow in hopes of dislodging the lump in his throat. "It's...nothing I expected. But despite what was going on, with you I've had moments of being happier than I've ever been in my life."

She lifted her head from his shoulder, blinking away the last of the tears.

He hoped the last of them.

"Once you find out how *average* I am, I'm afraid you'll change your mind."

Adam laughed. She was afraid *he'd* change his mind?

"Not happening," he said with complete confidence.

A smile trembled on her lips, warming him inside. "Okay."

Adam didn't have much familiarity with exhilaration, but he understood what he was feeling. Cupping her cheek with one hand, he said, "Do we have a deal?"

Now her smile could light the world. "Absolutely."

Too damn close to tears himself, he kissed her. Every time he could make love with her would help him survive the days or weeks he'd have to do without her. But after a moment he lifted his head so he could look at her. Just look. And he realized he'd have expected to anticipate apprehension sitting in his belly like a lump of lead until he could get to Seattle to see her…but he was pretty confident he wouldn't have to suffer that much.

Because he trusted her.

He was laughing when he slid down in the bed and swung her up over him to sit astride. Her lips were curved, too, when they met his.

* * * * *

Get 4 FREE REWARDS!

We'll send you 2 FREE Books plus 2 FREE Mystery Gifts.

Harlequin Romantic Suspense books are heart-racing page-turners with unexpected plot twists and irresistible chemistry that will keep you guessing to the very end.

FREE Value Over $20

YES! Please send me 2 FREE Harlequin Romantic Suspense novels and my 2 FREE gifts (gifts are worth about $10 retail). After receiving them, if I don't wish to receive any more books, I can return the shipping statement marked "cancel." If I don't cancel, I will receive 4 brand-new novels every month and be billed just $4.99 per book in the U.S. or $5.74 per book in Canada. That's a savings of at least 13% off the cover price! It's quite a bargain! Shipping and handling is just 50¢ per book in the U.S. and $1.25 per book in Canada.* I understand that accepting the 2 free books and gifts places me under no obligation to buy anything. I can always return a shipment and cancel at any time. The free books and gifts are mine to keep no matter what I decide.

240/340 HDN GNMZ

Name (please print)

Address   Apt. #

City   State/Province   Zip/Postal Code

Email: Please check this box ☐ if you would like to receive newsletters and promotional emails from Harlequin Enterprises ULC and its affiliates. You can unsubscribe anytime.

Mail to the **Harlequin Reader Service:**
IN U.S.A.: P.O. Box 1341, Buffalo, NY 14240-8531
IN CANADA: P.O. Box 603, Fort Erie, Ontario L2A 5X3

Want to try 2 free books from another series? Call 1-800-873-8635 or visit www.ReaderService.com.

*Terms and prices subject to change without notice. Prices do not include sales taxes, which will be charged (if applicable) based on your state or country of residence. Canadian residents will be charged applicable taxes. Offer not valid in Quebec. This offer is limited to one order per household. Books received may not be as shown. Not valid for current subscribers to Harlequin Romantic Suspense books. All orders subject to approval. Credit or debit balances in a customer's account(s) may be offset by any other outstanding balance owed by or to the customer. Please allow 4 to 6 weeks for delivery. Offer available while quantities last.

Your Privacy—Your information is being collected by Harlequin Enterprises ULC, operating as Harlequin Reader Service. For a complete summary of the information we collect, how we use this information and to whom it is disclosed, please visit our privacy notice located at corporate.harlequin.com/privacy-notice. From time to time we may also exchange your personal information with reputable third parties. If you wish to opt out of this sharing of your personal information, please visit readerservice.com/consumerschoice or call 1-800-873-8635. **Notice to California Residents**—Under California law, you have specific rights to control and access your data. For more information on these rights and how to exercise them, visit corporate.harlequin.com/california-privacy.

HRS21R2

Get 4 FREE REWARDS!

We'll send you 2 FREE Books plus 2 FREE Mystery Gifts.

Harlequin Presents books feature the glamorous lives of royals and billionaires in a world of exotic locations, where passion knows no bounds.

FREE Value Over $20

YES! Please send me 2 FREE Harlequin Presents novels and my 2 FREE gifts (gifts are worth about $10 retail). After receiving them, if I don't wish to receive any more books, I can return the shipping statement marked "cancel." If I don't cancel, I will receive 6 brand-new novels every month and be billed just $4.55 each for the regular-print edition or $5.80 each for the larger-print edition in the U.S., or $5.49 each for the regular-print edition or $5.99 each for the larger-print edition in Canada. That's a savings of at least 11% off the cover price! It's quite a bargain! Shipping and handling is just 50¢ per book in the U.S. and $1.25 per book in Canada.* I understand that accepting the 2 free books and gifts places me under no obligation to buy anything. I can always return a shipment and cancel at any time. The free books and gifts are mine to keep no matter what I decide.

Choose one: ☐ **Harlequin Presents Regular-Print** (106/306 HDN GNWY) ☐ **Harlequin Presents Larger-Print** (176/376 HDN GNWY)

Name (please print)

Address   Apt. #

City   State/Province   Zip/Postal Code

Email: Please check this box ☐ if you would like to receive newsletters and promotional emails from Harlequin Enterprises ULC and its affiliates. You can unsubscribe anytime.

Mail to the **Harlequin Reader Service:**
IN U.S.A.: P.O. Box 1341, Buffalo, NY 14240-8531
IN CANADA: P.O. Box 603, Fort Erie, Ontario L2A 5X3

Want to try 2 free books from another series? Call 1-800-873-8635 or visit www.ReaderService.com.

---

*Terms and prices subject to change without notice. Prices do not include sales taxes, which will be charged (if applicable) based on your state or country of residence. Canadian residents will be charged applicable taxes. Offer not valid in Quebec. This offer is limited to one order per household. Books received may not be as shown. Not valid for current subscribers to Harlequin Presents books. All orders subject to approval. Credit or debit balances in a customer's account(s) may be offset by any other outstanding balance owed by or to the customer. Please allow 4 to 6 weeks for delivery. Offer available while quantities last.

Your Privacy—Your information is being collected by Harlequin Enterprises ULC, operating as Harlequin Reader Service. For a complete summary of the information we collect, how we use this information and to whom it is disclosed, please visit our privacy notice located at corporate.harlequin.com/privacy-notice. From time to time we may also exchange your personal information with reputable third parties. If you wish to opt out of this sharing of your personal information, please visit readerservice.com/consumerschoice or call 1-800-873-8635. **Notice to California Residents**—Under California law, you have specific rights to control and access your data. For more information on these rights and how to exercise them, visit corporate.harlequin.com/california-privacy.

HP21R2

Get 4 FREE REWARDS!

We'll send you 2 FREE Books plus 2 FREE Mystery Gifts.

FREE Value Over **$20**

Both the **Romance** and **Suspense** collections feature compelling novels written by many of today's bestselling authors.

YES! Please send me 2 FREE novels from the Essential Romance or Essential Suspense Collection and my 2 FREE gifts (gifts are worth about $10 retail). After receiving them, if I don't wish to receive any more books, I can return the shipping statement marked "cancel." If I don't cancel, I will receive 4 brand-new novels every month and be billed just $7.24 each in the U.S. or $7.49 each in Canada. That's a savings of up to 28% off the cover price. It's quite a bargain! Shipping and handling is just 50¢ per book in the U.S. and $1.25 per book in Canada.* I understand that accepting the 2 free books and gifts places me under no obligation to buy anything. I can always return a shipment and cancel at any time. The free books and gifts are mine to keep no matter what I decide.

Choose one: ☐ **Essential Romance**
(194/394 MDN GQ6M) ☐ **Essential Suspense**
(191/391 MDN GQ6M)

Name (please print)

Address   Apt. #

City   State/Province   Zip/Postal Code

Email: Please check this box ☐ if you would like to receive newsletters and promotional emails from Harlequin Enterprises ULC and its affiliates. You can unsubscribe anytime.

Mail to the **Harlequin Reader Service:**
IN U.S.A.: P.O. Box 1341, Buffalo, NY 14240-8531
IN CANADA: P.O. Box 603, Fort Erie, Ontario L2A 5X3

Want to try 2 free books from another series! Call 1-800-873-8635 or visit www.ReaderService.com.

*Terms and prices subject to change without notice. Prices do not include sales taxes, which will be charged (if applicable) based on your state or country of residence. Canadian residents will be charged applicable taxes. Offer not valid in Quebec. This offer is limited to one order per household. Books received may not be as shown. Not valid for current subscribers to the Essential Romance or Essential Suspense Collection. All orders subject to approval. Credit or debit balances in a customer's account(s) may be offset by any other outstanding balance owed by or to the customer. Please allow 4 to 6 weeks for delivery. Offer available while quantities last.

Your Privacy—Your information is being collected by Harlequin Enterprises ULC, operating as Harlequin Reader Service. For a complete summary of the information we collect, how we use this information and to whom it is disclosed, please visit our privacy notice located at corporate.harlequin.com/privacy-notice. From time to time we may also exchange your personal information with reputable third parties. If you wish to opt out of this sharing of your personal information, please visit readerservice.com/consumerschoice or call 1-800-873-8635. **Notice to California Residents**—Under California law, you have specific rights to control and access your data. For more information on these rights and how to exercise them, visit corporate.harlequin.com/california-privacy.

STRS21R2

Get 4 FREE REWARDS!

We'll send you 2 FREE Books plus 2 FREE Mystery Gifts.

Worldwide Library books feature gripping mysteries from "whodunits" to police procedurals and courtroom dramas.

FREE Value Over $20

YES! Please send me 2 FREE novels from the Worldwide Library series and my 2 FREE gifts (gifts are worth about $10 retail). After receiving them, if I don't wish to receive any more books, I can return the shipping statement marked "cancel." If I don't cancel, I will receive 4 brand-new novels every month and be billed just $6.24 per book in the U.S. or $6.74 per book in Canada. That's a savings of at least 22% off the cover price. It's quite a bargain! Shipping and handling is just 50¢ per book in the U.S. and $1.25 per book in Canada.* I understand that accepting the 2 free books and gifts places me under no obligation to buy anything. I can always return a shipment and cancel at any time. The free books and gifts are mine to keep no matter what I decide.

414/424 WDN GNNZ

Name (please print)

Address   Apt. #

City   State/Province   Zip/Postal Code

Email: Please check this box ☐ if you would like to receive newsletters and promotional emails from Harlequin Enterprises ULC and its affiliates. You can unsubscribe anytime.

Mail to the **Harlequin Reader Service:**
IN U.S.A.: P.O. Box 1341, Buffalo, NY 14240-8531
IN CANADA: P.O. Box 603, Fort Erie, Ontario L2A 5X3

Want to try 2 free books from another series? Call 1-800-873-8635 or visit www.ReaderService.com.

*Terms and prices subject to change without notice. Prices do not include sales taxes, which will be charged (if applicable) based on your state or country of residence. Canadian residents will be charged applicable taxes. Offer not valid in Quebec. This offer is limited to one order per household. Books received may not be as shown. Not valid for current subscribers to the Worldwide Library series. All orders subject to approval. Credit or debit balances in a customer's account(s) may be offset by any other outstanding balance owed by or to the customer. Please allow 4 to 6 weeks for delivery. Offer available while quantities last.

Your Privacy—Your information is being collected by Harlequin Enterprises ULC, operating as Harlequin Reader Service. For a complete summary of the information we collect, how we use this information and to whom it is disclosed, please visit our privacy notice located at corporate.harlequin.com/privacy-notice. From time to time we may also exchange your personal information with reputable third parties. If you wish to opt out of this sharing of your personal information, please visit readerservice.com/consumerschoice or call 1-800-873-8635. **Notice to California Residents**—Under California law, you have specific rights to control and access your data. For more information on these rights and how to exercise them, visit corporate.harlequin.com/california-privacy.

WWL21R2

HARLEQUIN SELECTS COLLECTION

19 FREE BOOKS IN ALL!

From Robyn Carr to RaeAnne Thayne to Linda Lael Miller and Sherryl Woods we promise (actually, GUARANTEE!) each author in the Harlequin Selects collection has seen their name on the *New York Times* or *USA TODAY* bestseller lists!

YES! Please send me the **Harlequin Selects Collection**. This collection begins with 3 FREE books and 2 FREE gifts in the first shipment. Along with my 3 free books, I'll also get 4 more books from the Harlequin Selects Collection, which I may either return and owe nothing or keep for the low price of $24.14 U.S./$28.82 CAN. each plus $2.99 U.S./$7.49 CAN. for shipping and handling per shipment*.If I decide to continue, I will get 6 or 7 more books (about once a month for 7 months) but will only need to pay for 4. That means 2 or 3 books in every shipment will be FREE! If I decide to keep the entire collection, I'll have paid for only 32 books because 19 were FREE! I understand that accepting the 3 free books and gifts places me under no obligation to buy anything. I can always return a shipment and cancel at any time. My free books and gifts are mine to keep no matter what I decide.

☐ 262 HCN 5576   ☐ 462 HCN 5576

Name (please print)

Address   Apt. #

City   State/Province   Zip/Postal Code

Mail to the Harlequin Reader Service:
IN U.S.A.: P.O. Box 1341, Buffalo, NY 14240-8531
IN CANADA: P.O. Box 603, Fort Erie, Ontario L2A 5X3

*Terms and prices subject to change without notice. Prices do not include sales taxes, which will be charged (if applicable) based on your state or country of residence. Canadian residents will be charged applicable taxes. Offer not valid in Quebec. All orders subject to approval. Credit or debit balances in a customer's account(s) may be offset by any other outstanding balance owed by or to the customer. Please allow 3 to 4 weeks for delivery. Offer available while quantities last. © 2020 Harlequin Enterprises ULC. ® and ™ are trademarks owned by Harlequin Enterprises ULC.

Your Privacy—Your information is being collected by Harlequin Enterprises ULC, operating as Harlequin Reader Service. To see how we collect and use this information visit https://corporate.harlequin.com/privacy-notice. From time to time we may also exchange your personal information with reputable third parties. If you wish to opt out of this sharing of your personal information, please visit www.readerservice.com/consumerchoice or call 1-800-873-8635. Notice to California Residents—Under California law, you have specific rights to control and access your data. For more information visit https://corporate.harlequin.com/california-privacy.

50BOOKHS22R